Wagons West of Hell

Following the death of its guide, a wagon train bound for Gun Creek had stalled outside the small town on Conchita. But when Shane Preston and Jonah Jones rode in on the trail of the scar-faced man Shane had sworn to kill, wagon master Huston Whittaker saw an answer to their problems. Whittaker was an old friend of Shane's, and when he asked for help in getting his emigrants to their destination, the black-clad gunfighter and his crusty old sidekick couldn't refuse.

The trail ahead was going to be mighty hard, though. Somewhere out in the vast wilderness, a band of renegade Cheyennes were on the warpath. And there was no shortage of problems right inside the wagon train itself. A killer with a price on his head was trying to work his way west to a new life. A fiery half-Mexican girl on the run from a vengeful husband set her cap for the preacher who hoped to bring religion to Gun Creek. And three men masquerading as prospectors were planning a double-cross that would send the wagons and their occupants straight to hell!

Wagons West of Hell

Cole Shelton

A Black Horse Western

ROBERT HALE

First published by Cleveland Publishing Co. Pty Ltd,
New South Wales, Australia
First published in 1967
© 2020 Mike Stotter and David Whitehead

This edition © The Crowood Press, 2020

ISBN 978-0-7198-3125-6

The Crowood Press
The Stable Block
Crowood Lane
Ramsbury
Marlborough
Wiltshire SN8 2HR

www.bhwesterns.com

Robert Hale is an imprint
of The Crowood Press

ONE

SCARFACE TRAIL

They came out of the deep, pine-dotted canyon with thick red dust clinging to the sweat of their horses.

They rode swiftly, heading away from the long shadows of the pumice walls to where a contorted rim presided over another valley. The tall man came first, a lean, rugged streak with his leathery face set towards the western ridges. Right behind him, his oldster pard muttered curses at the weary mare he was prodding along.

The riders moved across the rim, and it was Shane Preston, the younger man, who reined in first. Sitting saddle, he let his cold eyes rove the length of the valley below. It was a vast basin carved out of the pumice, stretching into the dying sun and matted and tangled forests. Right at the far end, a river gushed over the rock wall and plunged into the valley, and even from this promontory, Shane could hear the distant roar.

"Another coupla hours and it'll be dark," Jonah Jones hinted as he drew alongside his companion.

Shane's eyes picked out the trail below them. It dropped from the rim down a huge rock staircase and wound like a thin ribbon through the darkening pines.

"And it's another two days and nights to Conchita," Shane reminded him. "That's if we keep riding."

"Aw—hell!" Jonah wheezed. "We haven't slept for three nights!"

"You'll have plenty of time for shuteye at Conchita," Shane said.

Jonah fingered his shaggy white beard and frowned.

"Shane," the old-timer said seriously, "don't go settin' your hopes too high."

"What do you mean?" Shane Preston asked him sharply.

"There are a helluva lot of scar-faced hombres on the frontier," the older gunfighter said. "This one at Conchita mightn't be the bastard who killed your wife."

Shane fixed his eyes on his pard. They were deepset, piercing eyes, the kind which seemed to look right through a man.

"Maybe not," the tall rider conceded softly. "But there was a report of a Scarface at Conchita, a real hardcase by all accounts, and I've no choice but to check him out."

"Sure," Jonah Jones shrugged, "I agree, Shane. But I've been watchin' you ever since you left Blacksmith County. You don't sleep, you hardly eat, and all that matters is reachin' Conchita. Seems you've set your heart on a showdown, and it's gonna be one helluva let-down if this Scarface ain't your man."

Shane turned his face away. There had been many false leads since the fateful day when he'd come home to find his wife murdered. Let-downs had become commonplace, the anticipated specter which haunted the end of every trail. And yet he had to keep on riding, driven by hate, nurtured by the hope that the next sundown would see the end of his quest—Scarface sprawled dead at his feet.

The tall gunfighter urged Snowfire towards the head of the trail. The big palomino ran easily, its magnificent white mane flowing wild and free in the late afternoon breeze. Behind this stallion came Jonah's old mare, Tessie, a horse which had seen better days long before her rider had met up with Shane, and that was three years ago. Now Jonah kept up a constant running battle with her, cursing, cajoling, and occasionally kicking the mare with his boot to keep up with his pard. Predictably, Shane had suggested trading Tessie for a more spritely mount, but Jonah had stubbornly refused to get rid of the horse. For a hardened gun hawk, Jonah could be strangely sentimental.

The trail clung to the sheer rock like an eyebrow, forcing the two gunfighters to ride single file. The tall man sat erect in the saddle, his steady hands in full control of his horse. He cast a long shadow, and the stark black of his shirt and Levis stood in sharp contrast against the fading red of the valley wall. Jonah Jones, however, presented a far more flamboyant figure. He was pudgy, white-haired, and dressed in a vivid blue vest and a pair of new check pants he'd spent ten bucks on back in Blacksmith County.

Shane reached the foot of the slope.

Without waiting, he flicked his rein and Snowfire headed along the narrow trail that twisted through a bunch of cedars. He was in the needle shadow of the first tree when a whip-crack sounded above the distant thunder of the falls, followed by a high-pitched scream that made Shane rein in, instantly.

"My God!" Jonah gulped as he drew alongside. "That sounded like—like a dang—"

"A woman's scream, Jonah," Shane Preston supplied.

The whip whistled again, but this time the gunfighters only heard a low moan instead of the frantic scream.

"Down-trail," Shane said aside to Jonah. "Just through those cedars. We'll take a look-see."

Jonah was about to mumble that maybe this was none of their business, but Shane was already guiding Snowfire between two towering trees. The thick bed of loam and pine needles muffled the sound of their horses' hoofs, and gloom enveloped them as they rode under the dark roof of interlaced branches. The gunfighters slowed their mounts as a sharp staccato of voices came to them, and Shane, riding just ahead, suddenly reined in.

The tall rider slid from his palomino and parted the branches.

The sinking sun was filtering through the trees, its fading light playing over the clearing. Right in the center of the hollow were three men, their backs to Shane, and looking past them, the gunfighter saw the object of their attention. A girl with long raven hair had her roped wrists lashed to the lowest branch of a gaunt cedar. The back of her blouse had been ripped away, exposing her bronze skin and two bloodied cuts that sliced from her right shoulder-blade almost to the base of her spine. She was groaning softly, her whole pain-wracked body trembling.

One of the men stepped towards her. He was a squat, frog-like figure, and Shane saw him slowly uncoil the long bull-whip in his hand. His two companions stood by watching, and one of them was casually rolling a cigarette.

"I reckon just one more lash, Juanita." The stumpy individual addressed the limp figure of the girl as he stood measuring her bare back. "Then I figure you'll have learned your lesson!"

The captive girl whipped her face around, and Shane saw the flash of hatred in her dark eyes and the scorn which curved her lips.

"Learn my lesson?" she gasped as the twin rivers of blood trickled to the waistband of her fringed buckskin skirt.

"So you think that whipping me will stop me from running away! You're a fool, Matt! I'll run the first chance I get!"

Jonah dropped down beside the tall gun hawk.

"Know something, boys?" The stocky individual smirked at his two companions. "I reckon she needs to be taught a *real* lesson! Maybe I'll fix it so she won't be able to even stand up, let alone ride away from me!"

"Do what you like," the red-haired man shrugged as he dragged on his cigarette. "After all, Woolrich, she's your wife."

"Wife!" Juanita echoed. "I was never a real wife to him, Hayter! I don't sleep with rattlesnakes!"

"Ah, for God's sake, Matt—get on with it," the other man said. He was a lean, ferret-faced ranny and he stomped impatiently over to his waiting horse to grab a whisky bottle.

The stumpy one raised his bull-whip, and the long lash was poised in his hand. Juanita stared defiantly at her husband, then turned her face against the cedar trunk as the whip described a practice flick over the pine needles. The bow-legged man with the leather measured up her glistening back.

"Hold it!" Shane's brittle command rang out over the clearing.

The two gunfighters shoved the branches apart and stepped together out of the foliage. Shane's black-handled six-shooter was clenched in his hand, while the old-timer clutched his .45 and the long Winchester he had taken from his saddle sheath. Bewildered and gaping, the three men simply stared as the strangers held them at gunpoint.

"Who—who in the hell are you?" the man with the whip sputtered furiously.

"Mister," Shane snapped. "Drop that whip!"

"Now listen here, whoever you are." Woolrich composed himself. "This ain't none of your business and you ain't welcome! Now get the hell outa here!"

"The whip, mister!" Shane reminded him.

There was something about the way Shane spoke that seemed to unnerve Woolrich. Slowly, he opened his fingers and the whip slithered down like a snake.

"Jonah," Shane directed his older partner, "cut the lady down."

"Like hell!" Juanita's husband snarled, barring his way.

"Listen—both of you! What's goin' on here is my business, and only mine—"

"When a lady gets bullwhipped I make it my business," Shane told him bluntly.

"For Pete's sake!" the other croaked. "This is between man and wife!"

"Where I come from, we don't use bull-whips," Shane said wryly. "Go ahead, Jonah."

The bearded gun hawk strode right up to Matt, whose bloated face was red with fury. Still the husband barred the way, but Jonah jabbed the muzzle of the Winchester into his flabby belly and gave him a choice.

"Either you step outa my way, hombre—or I'll *blast* you out!"

"You—you interferin' skunks!" the frog-like man grated.

"I told you—this is between me and my wife—"

Nevertheless, he stepped sideways and Jonah sauntered up to the prisoner. The gunfighter drew out his long hunting knife and slashed the rope that held her wrists to the branch. Juanita held out her bound wrists, and Jonah carefully cut through the ropes.

The gun in Shane's fist was rock-steady. "Ma'am—what's your side of the story?"

Juanita glanced defiantly at her husband. "I was running out on him! I had to go because of the things he wanted to do with me!"

"Juanita!" Matt rasped. "What happened in our marriage is private between you and me. It's not for the ears of damn strangers!"

"I made a mistake in marrying Matt Woolrich," Juanita flashed. "The biggest mistake in my life. He never cared for me, he was a drunkard, and he spent his time with the likes of—of these polecats with him now. I stood it all, even tried to be a good wife to him, but then—then—"

"Button up, Juanita!" Woolrich snarled.

"Go on, ma'am," Shane countered.

"He wanted me to sell my body," she snapped. "He wanted to make me into a common whore to earn filthy money to pay off his gambling debts. He was no good, so I left him, rode as far as I could. An hour ago he and his men caught up with me and—"

"And decided to teach you a lesson, huh?" Shane concluded.

Juanita was rubbing her wrists, trying to restore the circulation.

"Right!" Woolrich smirked at Shane. "So you know the story of our marriage! So what?"

"You must be the worst kind of buzzard, mister," old Jonah spat out. "Makin' your wife sell herself just to pay off gambling debts!"

Woolrich snickered. "Listen here ole goat! Juanita's a breed. Half-Mexican, half-Indian—and all breed women are whores!"

Juanita's right hand slapped hard across Woolrich's cheek, bringing the blood to his skin. His head flopped sideways and the girl prepared to vent her venom on him again.

"Ma'am," Shane Preston's upraised hand arrested her, "what do you want to do from here?"

"What does she want to do?" Matt Woolrich cried. "Hell, man! She comes with me! I happen to be her husband and she belongs to me! Maybe I did act a mite hasty in whipping her, but—"

"Mister!" Juanita was no longer defiant, but suddenly pleading. "Don't leave me here! Not with these—these polecats! Take me with you—anywhere—I don't care, as long as it's away from these pig-dogs!"

"Don't worry, ma'am," Shane assured her. "We won't be leaving you here, and as far as I'm concerned, you can come with us."

At first Jonah Jones gulped, then he nodded his approval as a smile of gratitude sprang to Juanita's lips.

"You—you goddamn wife-stealers!" Woolrich fumed, his eyes bright with anger.

"We ain't stealing her, Woolrich," Shane Preston said. "She's free to ride away from us any time she wants. In fact, we're only taking her to safety, and then she's on her own. If she wants to, she can even ride back to you."

"Never!" Juanita assured him.

"Ma'am," Shane said, "which one's your horse?"

"The pinto."

"Jonah," the tall gunslinger murmured, "fetch the lady's horse."

Matt Woolrich stared at him, stunned that this black-garbed stranger was going through with it. His mouth dropped open and he shook with rage as he watched Jonah heading towards Juanita's pinto pony, and suddenly his anger erupted.

"Take them!" he screamed.

Hayter's hand plunged downwards for his gun, and the ferret-faced man dodged to one side, drawing from his hip. Two guns boomed in deadly unison. Shane's bullet smashed into the ferret-faced man's chest, boring into his heart, lifting him clean off the ground and plastering him against the whipping-tree. Hayter had his gun clear of the holster, but even before he could level it, Jonah's bullet was blowing a hole right in the center of his forehead. Speechless and motionless, Matt Woolrich saw his two partners pitch forward and drop like sacks at his feet.

"You next, Woolrich?" Shane Preston demanded as the thin gray smoke drifted from his gun muzzle.

"Who—who *are* you?" Woolrich whispered, fear mingling with his anger.

"Shane Preston and Jonah Jones," the tall gun hawk introduced the pair of them.

"I'm damned!" Woolrich drew in his breath as he recalled a legend he'd heard in more than one saloon. "Preston and Jones, huh—two gunfighters! Well, Juanita, do you know just who you're riding off with? Two of the scum of the territory—two vultures who hire out their guns for cash!"

There was no fear in the half-breed girl's eyes as she surveyed Shane Preston, only wide-eyed interest.

"Whoever they are," Juanita informed her husband, "I'm riding with them."

Jonah led her pony past Woolrich, walking it to the edge of the clearing.

"You might be a coupla gun hawks," Woolrich grated. "But you'll pay for this!"

"Any time you're ready, Woolrich," Shane invited him.

Juanita regarded her husband with scorn. "He won't draw, Mr. Preston. Matt never takes part in a fair fight. The only time he fires on a man is from ambush or behind him!"

"Thanks for letting me know, ma'am," Shane said wryly. "Reckon we'll make durn sure he won't be coming along behind us in the near future."

Shane nodded to his partner.

"Run off their horses?" Jonah asked him.

"Yeah." Shane paced right up to Woolrich and extended his right hand to his holster. He whipped out the squat man's gun and stuck it into his own belt. "I want them so spooked that our friend here won't find them for days."

"You—you can't do this!" Matt Woolrich whimpered fearfully. "This is Cheyenne country! Hell, if those redskins see me without a horse and gun, they'll kill me!"

Shane ignored him, letting his frank eyes rove over the girl. She was a tall, slim figure with raven hair splashing over shoulders that had been made bare when Woolrich ripped her blouse Shane surveyed the torn garment thoughtfully.

"You'll find my horse the other side of those trees, ma'am," the gunfighter told her. "It's the palomino, and there's a spare shirt in my saddlebag if you haven't got any other clothes to wear."

"Thank you," Juanita said gratefully. "I left in such a hurry that I didn't bring any more than I'm dressed in now."

Jonah untethered the three horses ridden by Woolrich and his cronies and walked them out of the clearing. Seconds later, Shane heard his pard whooping and yelling and shooting like a wild man. There was a terrified whicker, then the frantic thunder of hoofs.

Meanwhile, Juanita ran to the other side of the clearing and disappeared behind the trees.

"I don't get it," Woolrich shook his head. "From what I heard, you two are only interested in chores with big money on the end. Why bother yourself over a damn breed girl—unless you've got *other* things in mind?"

Shane ignored the insinuation, merely holding his gun on Woolrich until the oldster stalked back into the clearing.

"Reckon those horses will be still going like bats outa hell at sundown," Jonah said proudly.

The branches parted and Juanita stepped into view. Shane held back a grin as his eyes took in the unglamorous black shirt that was several sizes too big for her. It flopped shapelessly where she'd tucked it in the waistband of her skirt, but even so, the garment failed to conceal the soft curves of her breasts.

Not so discreet as his younger pard, Jonah Jones failed to hold back a gleeful guffaw. Juanita glared at him momentarily, then she obeyed Shane's soft command and walked with the old-timer to the horses.

Shane stooped down and took the guns from the dead men. He backed to the edge of the clearing. Cold sweat was beading Woolrich's brow as he glanced around him at the friendless rocks and the towering trees of the wilderness. Shane took one of the guns and emptied the chamber. He tossed the

18

gun into the ferns, leaving Woolrich at least a slim chance of survival. Moments later, Shane was in the saddle and riding away with Jonah and the breed girl.

The campfire was like a big yellow tongue leaping into the night and throwing out a flickering glow. Shane had heaped three hefty logs onto the fire and now its warmth spread over the travelers as they sat around drinking the coffee Juanita had just brewed.

"So you're heading to Conchita," she said.

"And that's where we'll drop you off, ma'am," Shane informed her. "Reckon you can make your own way from there."

Juanita looked at him over the rim of her coffee mug. He'd be in his early thirties, she decided, a decade older than herself. She wouldn't exactly call him handsome, but there was something about his rugged face and strong shoulders that stirred an elemental emotion deep within her. She'd never quite had this feeling when she looked at her husband and instinctively, she tried to suppress it.

"Thank you both for horning in," she said gratefully.

"And thank you for preparing chow and coffee, ma'am," Shane grinned. "It's not often Jonah and me enjoy a woman's touch around the cooking pot."

"Cooking's one of the chores I've been used to for many years," she said. "Even before I met Matt. You see, I was raised at San Carla Mission, taken in as a baby by the sisters, and when I was twelve, I was made to help in the kitchen."

"Your parents both dead?" Shane rolled a cigarette.

Her face was in shadow. "My father was a Mexican bandido—I never knew him. Ma died at Sand Creek."

"In the massacre?" Shane recalled old history as he struck his match.

"My brother told me about it when I was old enough to understand," she said. "The troopers swooped on our camp and burned the teepees to the ground as a reprisal for a war-party attack on Fort William. Ma was butchered with a hundred other women and old men, just shot down with rifles. Suma, my brother, hid me until the soldiers left, and next day Father Rameres found us both and took us in. I stayed at the mission until I was nineteen. They were good to me at San Carla, Mr. Preston. Taught me your language, and your ways, and all about your God."

Maybe there was just a hint of sarcasm in that last statement, but Shane let it pass.

"And Suma?"

"He was eight years old when I was a baby," Juanita said. "It was Suma who told me about both my parents."

"Did he leave with you?" Shane ashed his cigarette.

A faint smile crossed her bronze face. "No, Mr. Preston. Suma became a priest."

Shane drew on his cigarette, aware that Juanita was scrutinizing him across the fire.

"My husband said you were both gunslingers," the half-breed girl ventured.

"Uh-huh."

"And—and that means …?"

"We hire out our guns to the highest bidder, ma'am," Shane Preston said bluntly. He picked up his canteen and stood up, a towering figure in the fire glow. "There's a creek down-trail. Reckon I'll fill this up ready for the ride. We'll mosey out in about one hour."

"Huh?" Juanita gulped. "You mean, we're not resting for the night here?"

"No, ma'am," Shane growled. "This is just a two-hour rest for chow and coffee—and for our horses. Could be the last long rest till we make Conchita."

He strode away into the darkness, and the girl heard his heavy boots crunch the pine needles. Beside her, Jonah was leaning forward to pour himself another coffee.

"Mr. Jones," she prompted him, "it must be a real important appointment you have in Conchita."

Jonah stirred his coffee. "He might be ridin' there to kill a man, ma'am."

"For cash?" She shivered.

"Not this time," Jonah murmured. "If Scarface is the man he's lookin' for, then this will be on Shane's own account."

"Scarface?" she frowned, bewildered.

Jonah Jones sipped his coffee, relishing the hot brew.

"It ain't exactly a secret, ma'am," the old-timer shrugged, "so you might as well know about Shane Preston. Once he used to be a rancher. Not so long ago he had a small spread and a lovely wife, Grace. One day he came home to find his home busted into and Grace dead—murdered by a coupla hard cases who came to rob."

"How terrible!" Juanita whispered.

"He trailed them to a border saloon." Jonah cleared his throat. "Killed one of them but before he could level his gun on the second hardcase, the outlaw shot him in the belly. I happened to be around a coupla minutes later, and since there wasn't a doc for miles, I took Shane out to my camp and cut the slug outa him. We've kinda rode together ever since, ma'am, riding on the trail of the one hardcase Shane didn't manage to kill in that saloon."

"Scarface?" she asked.

"Yeah. Shane had a good look at him just before he was shot. He had a long scar down his left cheek, and funny kinda—well, crazy eyes. We don't know his name, but every time Shane hears of a man with a scar, he rides in just in case it's the killer who murdered his wife."

Juanita shuddered as she thought about the kind of life Shane Preston must lead. Even while she'd been talking to him by the campfire, she'd noticed the restlessness in his eyes, the aloofness of his manner.

"Sometimes we don't get a lead for months," Jonah grunted. "So while we're searchin' and askin' around, we hire out our guns. Sorta helps pay for food and ammunition, and also keeps us riding in the kinda circles Scarface could be in. He's an outlaw, and Shane figures that while we keep tangling with such there's a good chance we'll meet up with Scarface—somewhere."

"And if he finds this Scarface and kills him?" Juanita whispered. "What then?"

She felt a presence near her and glanced up fearfully. The tall gunslinger had returned silently to the edge of the fire glow. The dancing light was playing over the hardness of his chiseled face and the dark line of the sideburns that curved down to his firm jaw.

"What then?" Shane repeated her question. "Why, then I'll hang up my guns, ma'am." His voice sounded hollow in the night.

TWO

WESTWARD THE WAGONS!

"Scarface Scammell?" Sheriff Lew Hodder grinned proudly as he surveyed the lean stranger standing before his desk. "You're a mite late, mister. Scammell's dead. Shot him myself, I did—and not before time!"

Shane stared at the stocky little sheriff leaning back in his chair. Hodder was a red-faced, balding man with a one-day beard sprouting on his chin.

"When was this?" Shane demanded.

"Yesterday afternoon," the lawman grinned. "I'd just about had my fill of the buzzard! He'd gunned down Pete McQuird, then wounded Kid Porteous, and that's when I went over to the saloon to bring the hardcase in. He chose to pull a damn gun on me, and then, mister, I blasted him."

24

"Anyway," Hodder's lanky deputy, Dowley, asked, "what's it to you, mister?"

"I'm looking for a Scarface who killed my wife," Shane Preston said. "If this Scammell is the man, I'll know it's time to stop searching. Where's his grave?"

"Ain't dug yet," Deputy Dowley grunted. "Funeral's this afternoon. Not that it'll be much of a funeral because Scammell wasn't exactly the most popular man in Conchita. However, I suppose even a hard-case is entitled to a Christian burial."

"I want to see him," the gunfighter said quietly. It wasn't a command, but the way Shane said it made the two lawmen exchange wary glances. "I suppose he's over at the undertaker's."

"Just who *are* you, mister?" Sheriff Hodder wanted to know.

"The name's Shane Preston."

The deputy's eyes narrowed. He whispered something to Sheriff Hodder, then nodded to Shane.

"I'll take you over there, Preston."

Shane strode out onto the boardwalk, waiting for Deputy Sam Dowley to join him in the mid-morning sunlight. Conchita was a town spawned by the cattlemen who came to buy supplies, sell their beeves, eat, drink and cavort with the percentage girls in the street's seven saloons. It was a town which had swelled overnight from a collection of shacks to a thriving business community, and now Shane Preston stood watching as riders and shoppers thronged Front Street.

The deputy ambled outside.

The parlor's just past the Black Deuce," he mumbled.

The two men paced together up the center of the street. Farther down from the saloons, a lone wagon was being backed across the street, scattering shoppers as its skidding wheels splattered thick red mud over the boardwalks. Finally, the wagon was positioned out front of Conchita's main general store, leaving deep ruts.

"Emigrants," Deputy Dowley muttered. "Reckon they've come in for supplies before setting out for Gun Creek."

"Noticed a circle of wagons just outside town as we rode in," the gunfighter said, as they passed the first saloon.

"Been here for nearly a week now," Dowley told him. "Heard they had some sorta trouble out on the trail."

"It's a helluva trek to Gun Creek," Shane said.

"There's cheap land out there," the lawman shrugged. "That's if they ever make it."

"How do you mean?"

"A big bunch of Cheyennes jumped the Reservation last month," Dowley stated. "They're out there in the prairie country, sure enough, and a small wagon train like this'n might be a big temptation."

"Have they got hardware?"

"Probably only a few old army carbines," the law officer guessed. "But God help us if those Cheyennes ever get hold of anything more powerful!"

A row of garish saloons greeted Shane Preston with tinny music and the aroma of cheap rotgut. Right now, they shared only a handful of patrons, but Shane figured that come sundown these liquor houses would be bulging at the seams.

Wesley P. Wolf was the town's mortician, and his colorful establishment was on the corner past the Black Deuce Saloon. Outside, a blue notice board nailed over his door announced that in addition to supplying a dignified burial service, Wesley P. Wolf also hand-carved headstones, crosses and made the best coffins in Wyoming.

Deputy Sam Dowley pushed open the door, and a round face popped up from behind a stack of pine boxes.

"'Mornin', Sam," Wolf said, his face glowing in anticipation. "You've come to bring me some business?"

Wesley P. Wolf was as colorful as his parlor's exterior. He wore a frilly white shirt, with a dandy's string tie dangling beneath his double chin, and apart from

27

the undertaker's traditional pin-striped pants, one might easily mistake him for a tinhorn gambler.

"Not today, Wesley," Dowley grinned. "Don't forget we brought you some yesterday afternoon."

"Scammell!" Wesley P. Wolf spat in disgust. "I sure wouldn't get rich on the likes of him! No kin, no money—a pauper's funeral paid for by the town!"

"It's about Scammell that we're here," Dowley said. "This gent wants to see him."

Wolf afforded Shane a hopeful glance. "You're a relative maybe, or a friend of Mr. Scammell? Well, perhaps you'd like to pay for a very special funeral for him. Now, a really good Wesley P. Wolf special funeral with all the trimmings costs only twenty dollars but if you can't afford that, there's another one at fifteen dollars—"

"I didn't come to pay for Scammell's funeral," Shane said, pushing his way past the stacked coffins.

"Oh," Wolf's smile vanished.

"Where is he?" Shane demanded.

Wolf frowned. "Well, he's out back, of course."

"I'll follow you, Mr. Wolf," the gunfighter said. "I want the coffin opened up."

"But—but that's hardly ethical," the undertaker gulped his protest.

Shane fumbled in his hip pocket and withdrew a leather wallet. He counted five one-dollar bills and placed them on top of Wolf's deluxe model coffin.

"Would these make it a mite more ethical?"

Wesley P. Wolf smiled, his principles suddenly gone. "Well, I daresay you've a right to view the deceased."

The mortician stuffed the money into his fob pocket and led the way through the pine box maze. He unlocked a door, and a musty aroma greeted Shane as he ducked low and followed Wolf into the gloom. Wolf reached for a candle and handed it to the gunslinger.

A match flared in the darkness and found the wick.

A solitary casket reposed along the far wall. It was a plain, unpainted box made of crude pine, and Shane felt coldness creep over him as he held the light for the mortician. This could be the end of the trail, the culmination of years of hate. The man who killed Grace could be right here at his feet.

Wesley P. Wolf stooped down and the flickering flame made weird shadows on the drab walls. He began to prise open the lid and Shane heard the creak of protesting nails.

"Here, take a look for yourself," Wolf said when the lid was raised.

Shane squatted down and thrust the candle into the coffin.

The body lay long and still beneath him. Arms and legs were as straight as pegs, and as Shane pushed the candle farther into the casket, he saw the dead man's face. It was white and sallow, and the eyes were open and staring sightlessly up at the flame. A long, deep scar marred his face, curling right to the corner of lips that had turned blue. Shane gave him a cursory glance before he stood up.

"Well?" Wesley P. Wolf asked expectantly.

"Thanks for opening the coffin," Shane grunted.

He stood back as Wolf lowered the lid.

Shane blew out the candle and handed it back to the mortician. He gave the deputy a brief nod and weaved his way among the coffins back onto the street. Leaving the smell of death behind, he took a pace into the sunlight.

"You ain't saying much," Deputy Dowley commented, as he caught up.

"There's not much to say," Shane said, his voice even. "Scammell's not my man."

Shane Preston left the lawman frowning on the street as he strode away. He felt a strange relief within him, a burden suddenly lifted as he realized that Scarface was still alive and free. He hadn't wanted Scammell to be his man. It would have been a sour ending to years of sweat and gunfire, of long trails and false leads, to find his quarry killed by another man! Because Shane himself had to fire the bullet that killed Scarface—that was the only way he could find rest.

He spotted the horses down-street.

He had left the old-timer about to venture into the French Palace, and he figured right now on joining him.

Opposite their two horses, tethered to another tie-rail outside a rooming house, was Juanita's pinto pony. This was the parting of the ways as far as Juanita and the gunfighters were concerned, and Shane smiled to himself as he recalled how the half-breed girl had planted a wet kiss on Jonah's beard, then leaned over to give him a kiss of gratitude. It could have easily developed into the kind of kiss that might have persuaded most men to stay around for more, but Shane had gently pushed her away.

Leaving the deputy still scratching his head, Shane parted the batwings of the French Palace. The town's biggest saloon was a converted barn, with a high rafter-crossed ceiling from which hung six oil lamps. Most of the floor was taken up with poker tables, and as Shane made for the bar, he saw two games in progress. A pouting percentage girl smiled at him, then shrugged as he ignored her charms and walked to where the old-timer was drinking with another man. Even as he approached, Shane figured there was something familiar about Jonah's companion, despite the fact that he could see only the back of his head.

Hearing the crunch of Shane's boots, Jonah Jones angled his head around.

"His name was Scammell," Shane Preston announced as he stood beside the bar counter next to the oldster. "He's dead, Jonah, just some hardcase shot by the town lawman—not the buzzard I'm looking for."

For a long moment, Jonah Jones digested this piece of information.

Right then, the old-timer's drinking companion slowly turned his head.

"I don't reckon there's any need to introduce you two." Jonah lifted his glass of redeye.

"Huss Whittaker!" Shane grinned. "I knew I'd seen that woolly hair somewhere!"

The gaunt, smiling man extended a hand which the gunfighter gripped warmly.

"Been a long time, Shane," Whittaker stated. "And I'd have missed you but for that horse of yours. Knew Snowfire the moment I came outa the general store, and when I crossed over to stand by the horse, Jonah here saw me and came out to ask questions."

"Figured he might be tryin' to rustle your cayuse right on the street!" the old-timer said to Shane. "When Huss here convinced me he'd only good intentions, we decided on a friendly drink until you showed!"

Shane signaled the bartender.

"Drinks on me," the tall gunfighter said.

Jonah downed his drink in a single gulp and lined up his glass for the next round. The rangy old bar-keep, wearing a spotless white apron over his pants, sidled up to them.

"Bottle of whisky," Shane ordered. "Not the rot-gut my pards have been drinking, but the best in the house."

"Yes, sir!" the bartender grinned.

Shane turned to Huston Whittaker. "And what the heck are you doing in Conchita? We're a long ways from Rimrock!"

"We sold up the spread," Whittaker explained, "and bought ourselves a wagon. It's one of those just outa town, Shane. We're part of the wagon train heading west for Gun Creek, going there to start up fresh. Gun Creek's a new settlement just past Fort Defiance."

Shane stared at him in amazement. He'd known Huston Whittaker for years, and the leather-faced rancher had always seemed settled, hardly the wandering kind.

"Well," Shane said, raising his glass, "we'll drink to that new life you're heading to."

Whittaker hesitated.

"We might take some time to get there, Shane," he said seriously.

"Yeah?"

"Huss has just been tellin' me," Jonah said, sipping his rye. "There's been real trouble. His trail scout was killed just before they arrived at Conchita."

"Indians?" Shane asked.

"He was knifed," Huston Whittaker recalled. "Stabbed in the back right beside one of the wagons. Indians, probably, or maybe an outlaw he caught sneaking around. Fact is, the wagon train has no trail-scout, and that's why we haven't left Conchita. We've been hoping someone here will scout for us."

"Job pay well?" the tall gunfighter said.

"I'm the wagon master, Shane," Huston Whittaker informed him. "And last week when we arrived here, I called a meeting of all the emigrants and we decided to set aside four hundred bucks for the man—or men—who'd scout for us and bring us safe to Gun Creek."

"Well," Shane remarked, "you should have plenty of takers at that price."

Whittaker shook his head. "We had one, first day, but when he heard about the Cheyennes jumping the Reservation, he resigned before we could hitch up the wagons." Shane downed his drink and poured fresh ones. "Shane," Huston Whittaker's voice was soft, "Jonah told me about the man with the scar, and I heard you tell him the dead man wasn't the one you're looking for."

"Correct." Shane swirled the liquor in his glass.

"So right now you and Jonah are at a loose end," Whittaker concluded.

"We'll probably ride back to Blacksmith County," Shane Preston murmured. "That's our last forwarding address. Could be someone's written in for our services."

"How'd you like to ride back with four hundred bucks?" the wagon master asked him.

Shane looked at him, searching his old friend's face. Whittaker's craggy features were lined, betraying forty hard years, and Shane glimpsed the concern in his eyes.

"We ain't exactly trail scouts." Shane's brittle reply seemed to dash Whittaker's hopes.

"Jonah told me he used to ride civilian scout for the army," Huston Whittaker insisted. "And he happened to mention you've both been to Fort Defiance several times, so you'd know the trail."

"Maybe so," Shane Preston conceded. "But all that doesn't make us wagon train scouts! Look, Huss, you know damn well what we are. We're gunslingers, hired guns."

"Which makes you both damn good candidates for the scouting jobs," the wagon master jumped in quickly. "With outlaws on the prairie and maybe renegade Cheyennes as well, this wagon train ain't gonna be no Sunday School picnic."

"We—er—need the money," Jonah Jones reminded Shane. "We haven't been offered a job in months."

"Four hundred bucks, Shane," Wagon master Whittaker said.

Shane picked up his second drink. He and Jonah had taken on a variety of chores, from taming a town to helping sodbusters against greedy ranchers, and normally their work involved siding with folks where the law had failed. He'd never pictured them as trail scouts guiding pioneers to their Promised Land. And yet, four hundred dollars would come in mighty handy right now, and in addition, he'd be helping out a friend. There was a tense silence.

"We're gonna be a week on the trail," Shane Preston said. "So let's have a last whisky before we leave!"

"Folks," Huston Whittaker raised his hands high as they gathered around the water barrel he'd mounted, "we're ready to move out on account of we've hired ourselves two trail scouts!"

They stood around, hardy pioneer stock, men with long rifles standing alongside women and kids. Behind them, four wagons were motionless, and horses grazed beside goats, sheep, cows and a couple of steers. Washing hung limply on a line strung between two wagons, and when Whittaker began to make his speech, the last emigrant poked his head between a shirt and a woman's petticoat and ambled over to join the crowd listening expectantly to the wagon master.

"Meet Shane Preston and Jonah Jones." Whittaker indicated the two gunfighters sitting saddle. "I can vouch for them myself."

"That's good enough for us, Huss," a young man with corn-colored hair spoke up in a booming voice. He turned his fierce eyes on the riders. "Welcome to the Lord's wagon train—I'm Abel Sorenson."

"Preacher man," Huston Whittaker murmured, almost apologetically, as the two gunfighters fixed their eyes on the tall streak of a man with his shaggy, unkempt hair flopping about a boyish face.

"Heading west to build a House of God in Gun Creek," Sorenson declared. "They say it's the devil's own town, no sheriff, no law and order, no church! And I'm riding there to see that the Lord's will is done."

"Actually, Abel," a tubby man spoke up dryly, "I figure you might be exaggerating some."

"We shall see, Brett Craig," the preacher man proclaimed. "We shall see!"

Craig was a man in his late thirties, fluffy-haired, with wide brown eyes and a beard. He was squat, with a bull-neck and thickset shoulders. Beside him stood a demure little woman about his age, wearing steel-rimmed spectacles on the bridge of her nose. Two small lads, and a girl about seven clad in a smock, played around their parents.

"My wife, Janie," Brett Craig introduced the woman at his side.

"Glad to know you, ma'am," Shane smiled amicably.

"You know my wife, of course." Whittaker grinned at the tall, stately woman in the long blue dress and sunbonnet.

"Howdy, Gloria," Shane nodded. The Whittakers' son, Tim, scowled at him. He'd always been a precocious child, too cheeky for his tender years.

"Like you to meet three prospectors, Shane," Whittaker indicated a trio of men who stood together.

"Prospectors?" Jonah frowned.

"We've heard there's gold west of Gun Creek," a big, beefy man stated. "My name's Blake."

"Welcome to the wagons," Blake's bald-headed sidekick muttered. "I'm Morton."

The third member of the trio was smoking a pipe. He was a hard-bitten, lanky pioneer with protruding ears and thick, fleshy lips. Shane saw that he was carrying the latest Winchester repeating rifle in his hairy fist.

"Eli McKay," he introduced himself.

"Not exactly the biggest wagon train ever," Whittaker told the gunslingers. "In fact, we started out with two other families. Both of them stopped off on the way when they heard about the Cheyennes busting out of the Reservation."

"Reckon we've been waiting around here long enough, Huss," Blake growled. "Let's get these wagons moving!"

Whittaker turned to the gun hawks. "You ready?"

"Hitch the wagons," Shane Preston said.

The pioneers needed no second invitation. With the kids whooping like Indians, the wagoners stalked over to the horses which had just enjoyed a week's respite from the dust of the trail. Shane and Jonah watched as livestock were rounded up, water barrels strapped to wagons, horses backed into harness and furniture hastily stacked under the canvas.

For fully an hour, the settlers busied themselves preparing for the trail ahead, and the two gunfighters made their own brief preparations.

"Know something?" Jonah screwed up his face. "A coupla men on this wagon train seem, well, kinda familiar."

"Who for instance?" Shane asked him.

"I reckon I've seen several of those prospectors some place before," Jonah insisted. "But I can't remember where."

"I don't know any of them," Shane Preston shook his head. "But there's one other hombre here who's got a reward dodger out on him."

"*What?*" Jonah gaped.

Just then the sound of hoofs jerked their heads around, and the wagoners looked up from their chores as a rider surged up the grassy slope towards them. Huston Whittaker came and stood beside his scouts, waiting with them as the rider with long black hair slowed her pinto pony to a walk.

"Juanita!" Jonah exclaimed. "What the heck's she doin' here?"

"You know this lady?" Huston Whittaker asked them.

"You could say that," the tall gunfighter said dryly. Juanita had obviously been on a small buying spree in Conchita. She now wore a tight-fitting check shirt and Levis. Her pretty face was flushed from hard riding, and her young, firm bosom heaved tumultuously as she reined in.

"Howdy!" she smiled breathlessly at Shane and Jonah. "I'm looking for the wagon master!"

"That's me, Huss Whittaker," the gaunt pioneer stated, his hollow eyes moving appreciatively over the half-breed girl. "What can I do for you?"

Encouraged by this reception, Juanita decided to come straight to the point.

"Mr. Whittaker," she said, "I want to join your wagon train!"

Shane Preston reined in his horse.

He was on the rim of a high pumice-stone bluff that loomed over the grasslands below. Up here, the mid-afternoon sun blazed relentlessly down on him, and the hot wind whipped his rugged face. To the west, a haze obscured the distant ridges, but between the wagons and these craggy rocks lay the sprawling upland prairie, rolling grass and two deep rivers, a land with few trees. It was across this plateau that the wagons had to pass before they could cross the high country to their destination.

Shane drew on his cigarette as he turned his head eastwards. The prairie schooners were just about to round the bluff, their dusty white canvases billowing like sails in the wind. They lumbered along in line, Whittaker's wagon at the head. Just about all the wagons had cows or goats roped along behind, and sometimes the kids would jump down and whip the animals to make them walk faster and not drag on the ropes. Shane picked out old Jonah riding ahead with Huss Whittaker, and then his eyes drifted farther east until they rested on the distant houses of Conchita. Soon the town would be left behind, and the grassy wilderness would swallow up the pioneer train. The only other community between here and Fort Defiance was a little town called Gaucho. From this small prairie town to Fort Defiance, the terrain would rise sharply and the trek over the high country would be arduous. Once at the outpost, however, the wagons would be almost at journey's end. According to Whittaker, the primitive new settlement they were headed for was just west of the fort.

Shane surveyed the prairie trail once again, then turned the palomino down from the rim.

It was then that he glimpsed the rider.

Brett Craig had left the wagon train to climb the pumice bluff, and Shane reined in as the pioneer headed deliberately towards him. The man on the bay gelding came closer and Shane flicked the ash from his cigarette as he waited for him.

"Something wrong, Craig?" Shane Preston demanded as the rider drew alongside him.

The two riders were stark black silhouettes against the azure sky. Brett Craig's searching eyes were fixed on Shane's, and the scout noticed the pearl-handled .45 nestling in the man's holster.

"Why didn't you say something?" Brett Craig asked him.

Shane studied him for a moment, dragging on his cigarette.

"I can tell you know about me, Preston," the wagoner said bluntly. "I could see it in your eyes when we met. And from what I've heard about you, you kinda make it your business to know about men like me!"

"I'm not here to take you in, Craig," the gunfighter said.

Shane's reassurance didn't seem to relax the rider one bit. He fidgeted nervously.

"Then you've seen the 'wanted' dodgers?" he demanded.

"Like you said," Shane said wryly. "I make it my business to keep my eyes open."

"How much is on my head now?"

"Coupla hundred," Shane informed him casually.

"Those dodgers carry lies!" the emigrant croaked. "Goddamn lies!"

"Listen," Shane tossed away his cigarette, "just calm down, Craig. I know the story, and it's because I know it I said nothing back at Conchita. Doesn't it strike you that I could have talked up and earned myself a quick two hundred bucks by taking you in back there?"

Brett wiped the beads of perspiration from his brow, and his right hand drifted conspicuously away from his gun butt.

"It was a fair fight," Craig looked him square in the face. "Sure I killed Lucas Tramner, but it was a fair fight. Howsomever, it seems I'm to be branded outlaw because Tramner had a lot of influence in Tombstone. All Tramner's pards swore I murdered him, and I had to run from the law."

"That's how I heard it," Shane said.

"Figured that Gun Creek would be far enough west for me to start a new life," Craig said. "No one on the wagon train knows about me except you."

"Your secret's safe with me," Shane assured him.

Brett Craig stared at him, recalling all the things he'd heard about Shane Preston. Some of the legends which had stuck to his name were probably true—gunfighter, bounty hawk, town-tamer—but plainly he wasn't a man without feeling. Tentatively, Craig extended a hand which Shane gripped. Right there, on that windswept bluff, a strange bond was sealed between two men, the hunter and the hunted.

"Better head back to the wagons," Shane directed quietly.

"Sure."

By now the wagons had passed the bluff, and Whittaker's prairie schooner was nosing out into the sea of yellowing grass, heading for the Promised Land beyond the far range.

"Who found the dead scout?" Shane asked suddenly.

"Whittaker," Craig replied, flashing a swift look aside at the gunfighter. "Why?"

"Huss said he figured it was Indians," Shane probed.

"Maybe," Brett Craig murmured. They turned their horses down the narrow trail which dropped away from the bluff. "His name was Cutting, Jim Cutting, a damn fine scout. Whittaker found him with a knife between his shoulder blades just beyond the prospectors' wagon. It was early one morning, and we figured Jim had been dead most of the night."

"A Cheyenne knife?"

"Yeah," Brett Craig recalled. "But a lot of white men carry those knives now—the Reservation Indians sell them at the trading post."

"Just what are you trying to say?" Shane's eyes narrowed.

There was a long pause. "Maybe nothing."

"If Indians killed Cutting," Shane mused. "There's one question which comes to mind."

"What?"

"With the scout dead, why didn't they raid the wagon train—specially as it must have been dark, and folks inside their wagons?"

Craig appeared to want to change the subject. "You know, Preston, maybe I shouldn't be saying this, but there's one hombre on this wagon train who smells like trouble."

"Who's that?"

"Damien Blake."

"And Cutting's body was found outside Blake's wagon?" Shane twisted the question back to the subject.

"Jim Cutting and Blake had traded words more than once," Brett Craig told the gunfighter.

"What are you saying?" Shane repeated his earlier question.

Brett Craig swallowed. "I reckon we oughta get back to the wagons."

The fugitive spurred his gelding ahead, and Shane watched him thoughtfully as he headed down-trail to the grasslands. Then, slapping Snowfire with his rein, the gunfighter rode in his dusty wake.

"My child," Pastor Abel Sorenson frowned paternally on Juanita, "I certainly won't engage in such frivolity!"

"Oh, why not?" the half-breed girl laughed above the strains of Brett Craig's fiddle.

"Because," Sorenson said, "dancing is the devil's work."

"I see," she said meekly but there was still laughter in her eyes.

A big campfire blazed in the center of the wagon circle, and to one side, Craig was playing his squeaky violin. Almost instinctively, Juanita had started to jump around in time with the music, and soon Whittaker and his wife were dancing. Reb Morton had then grabbed the half-breed girl, and old Jonah Jones was led protestingly onto the dance floor by Janie Craig. The oldster danced like an elephant, but he seemed to be enjoying himself all the same.

"You know, Abel," said Juanita, breathless after her dances, "I'm so grateful to Huss Whittaker for letting me come along."

"When you said you'd cook for us all, how could he refuse?" the preacher man grinned. "And if tonight's chow was an example, our wagon master made a good choice."

Juanita's deep, flashing eyes roved over him with heightened interest. He might be a preacher, but he was a good-looking man as well. There was strength in his broad shoulders, resolution in his jutting jaw, and she liked the way his hair grew wild and free as the wind which blew through it. Abel Sorenson had a handsome face with a firm nose and full, almost sensuous lips.

"My child," Sorenson murmured, "I presume Huss Whittaker has—ah—made proper sleeping arrangements for you tonight?"

"I told him I'd sleep out under a wagon, or maybe by the fire," she told him.

Abel Sorenson looked aghast. "You mean—out in the open?"

"Where else?" Juanita spread her hands. "I don't own a wagon. Mind you, if someone I liked was to offer to share a wagon, then I might consider it."

Sorenson swallowed.

"Juanita!" he chided her. "You must not even dream of such things! And you certainly must not mention them to a man of the cloth!"

"Way I see it, Abel," she smiled, an unmistakable twinkle in her eyes. "A preacher's a man, like any other. The fact that he preaches makes no difference."

"But it makes *all* the difference!" There was an air of pomposity in Sorenson's voice.

Juanita's left foot was tapping in time with the music. She watched old Jonah Jones executing a jig to the accompaniment of clapping from the wagoners.

"Juanita," the preacher man ventured, "there's something I've been meaning to ask you all day. Just what is a young, single woman like you doing on a westbound wagon train?"

"Reckon I ought to put you straight about a few things, Abel." Juanita's toe was still tapping. "First, I'm not much younger than you. Second, I ain't single—"

Sorenson's face fell and she heard him draw in his breath.

"I'm a married woman, Abel, on the run from my husband."

"Husband!" he exclaimed.

"Lastly," she grinned, "you might be a preacher man, but on this frontier, it sometimes pays to mind your own business!"

He stared at her. "A husband!" he repeated.

"Yes, Preacher man," she said, delighting in teasing him. "An evil buzzard of a man!" She moved gaily away.

Pastor Sorenson compressed his lips. The fact that she was married definitely meant that any relationship between her and Preacher Abel Sorenson was stifled at the outset. A man of the cloth could have nothing to do with a woman running away from a marriage. He would have been surprised had he known what thoughts were passing through the girl's mind.

"Not getting on too well with the preacher man?" Damien Blake's hand snaked out of the darkness to grip her bare arm.

"Please! You're hurting me!"

Blake's bear-like figure barred her path, and the fire glow gave him a sinister look as he stared down at her.

"Reckon a purty little thing like you should be dancing—with a *real* man," Damien Blake smirked, his claw-like fingers still around her arm.

Even the smell of him revolted her. He had bulging eyes, a long hooked nose, and when he parted his lips, his broken, decaying teeth stood up like stunted yellow stumps. But she knew how to handle men.

She said, lightly, "Maybe later, huh?"

"What's wrong with now?" Blake growled.

He didn't wait for her answer. He hustled her over to where the others were dancing, and as Craig continued to play his violin, he clutched her close to his hefty body and began to jig around. After a time, Juanita tried to break away but he tried to kiss her and she wrenched her head to one side. Seeing her distress, Brett Craig stopped fiddling.

"Reckon it's time for a smoke," Brett said, reaching for his tobacco sack.

"Hell, no!" Damien Blake bellowed. "Everyone's just started to have fun. Start that fiddling again!"

Brett Craig hesitated.

"*Start playin'*!" Blake snarled. "Or I'll bust that fiddle over your head!"

Juanita watched a vein pulsing in Blake's temple. For a long moment, he glared at the musician, and in the silence Craig's eyes narrowed. Then, reluctantly, he picked up his violin. The music flowed from his moving bow, and Blake pulled Juanita hard against him as he danced her around, with his boots alternately crunching the ground and her feet. Trapped and miserable, Juanita had no choice but to allow him to enjoy the limp warmth of her body and to let his hand fondle the back of her hair.

Out of the shadows a man stepped.

"Ma'am," Shane Preston drawled, "didn't you promise me this dance?"

The music stopped.

"Why—yes, Mr. Preston," Juanita breathed gratefully. "I remember now. This one *was* yours!"

Blake fixed his dark, brooding eyes on the tall gunfighter.

"Just get the hell outa here, Preston," he grunted. "Me and the girl are dancin'."

"Didn't you hear her, Blake?" snapped Shane. "She saved this dance for me."

"Then where in hell were you?" Damien Blake challenged him.

"Checking the horse-lines," Shane said. "Maybe I arrived back a mite late, but that makes no difference. The dance is mine."

Damien Blake relaxed his grip on the girl, and in a moment, she wormed under his arm and stepped back from him. Breathing easier now, she moved over towards Shane.

"All right," Blake grated. "So this one's yours! But I'm linin' up for the next one. In fact, I might just dance with this little 'breed all night!"

"Forgot to tell you, Blake," Shane murmured. "Juanita's booked up for the night's dancing. After me there's Jonah, and then Huss Whittaker comes next on the list before I come in again. Of course, if Juanita wants to change things—" He let it hang.

"I want it just like that," she said quickly.

Damien Blake let his hand edge towards the brown butt of his six-shooter. His narrowed eyes burned like twin coals and his hand trembled with fury. Suddenly, Shane shoved the girl to one side, facing Blake squarely. There was a coldness in Shane's eyes and for a bleak moment Blake saw the gunfighter's stark challenge. He decided to bluff it out with a laugh. He planted his hands on his hips and bellowed out a loud guffaw.

"Who in hell wants to dance with a 'breed?" he roared, then turned on his heels and marched over to the whisky keg.

No one moved as Blake drew a mugful from the tap, but as the burly settler downed the drink with an exaggerated flourish, Craig played a few cautious bars on his violin and the dancing started up again.

"Thank you for rescuing me, Shane," Juanita murmured, as the gunfighter danced with her.

"I could see he was getting mean," Shane said.

Deliberately, the girl moved closer to the tall gunslick, and when his eyes met hers, she molded her soft body against his. Soon Brett Craig was in full swing, and the music floated out over the darkness of the prairie. As the music swelled, Juanita happened to glance over at Abel Sorenson's wagon. She grinned as she saw the preacher man's fingers drumming out the tune on the rim of one of the wheels. Then, as she danced around his side of the campfire, she whispered a word to Shane and he released her. She grabbed Abel Sorenson's hands. The preacher's mouth opened to protest, but the girl whirled him into the dance. At first, Sorenson looked around desperately, trying to escape, but as Craig's violin music turned into an infectious jig, the preacher began to prance in time. His sermonizing was forgotten, and as if mesmerized by Juanita's laughing eyes and the stomp of feet on the hard earth, Abel Sorenson lost his inhibitions. He even looked like he was enjoying himself.

"Quite a girl, Damien," Eli McKay remarked aside to Blake as they stood in the shadows between two wagons.

Blake drew on his cigarette and the glowing tip illuminated the angry frustration on his face.

"Yeah," Blake drawled softly. "And before I've finished with her, she'll be eating outa my hand."

"And Preston?"

"Eli." Damien Blake lowered his voice and now it carried a sinister ring. "Both of us know damn well what's gonna happen to Shane Preston—*the same as'll happen to everyone else on this wagon train!*"

THREE

RAW FISTS AT SUNUP

Abel Sorenson awoke with the dawn.

Yawning, he stretched beneath the blankets and looked sleepily up at the flapping canvas over his bunk. He could hear the rustle of the wind in the grass and a draught filtered into his wagon to ruffle his hair.

The preacher eased himself from the blankets and pulled on his pants. He'd bedded down between two large cases, the ones which held all his theological books. Just three months ago, he'd been a graduate from Bible College, with the choice of two well-paid pastoral jobs. Abel had rejected them both, feeling the call of the raw frontier where as yet there were no stately churches with plush pews. He was in effect a missionary.

And then he remembered last night.

At first, he felt a trifle ashamed of himself for joining in the dancing but he reminded himself that to become a successful pastor he had to be one with his people. His thoughts strayed to the half-breed girl. She was married, which closed the door on anything more than friendship with her. He'd have to keep his feelings for her a secret!

Abel Sorenson climbed down out of his wagon.

To the east, pink fingers of light were tipping the far rims and stretching out over the prairie grass. The preacher glanced at the dead fire in the center of the wagon square. Sprawled beside the charred logs lay old Jonah Jones, snoring loudly. As yet, the wagons were shrouded in silence, and Abel's eyes caught the only sign of movement just beyond the circle of wagons. Shane Preston was with his palomino.

Sorenson gazed north to where the flat prairie seemed to dip, and he remembered the creek that the wagons had been hauled across the night before. He decided on a cold water wash.

The preacher man was stripped to the waist as he strode through the grass. Halfway to the creek, he heard the sound of splashing. One of the other men was already there, he told himself.

Humming a hymn, he walked to the bank and peered down at the creek.

Right below him, a bronze, naked body was twisting and turning in the water, and Abel Sorenson froze in horror. A shapely form surfaced in a flurry of foam and the early morning light glistened on Juanita's copper-colored curves. Acutely embarrassed, Abel Sorenson stepped back in case she caught him watching her.

But just then he glimpsed another figure farther along the bank, a man crouching in the brush, watching intently. Momentarily stunned, Sorenson stared at Damien Blake as the hefty teamster's eyes feasted on the raven-haired beauty bathing in the creek. Righteous anger rose in the preacher's chest. Blake was edging closer to the bank, trying to get a better view.

"Mr. Blake!" The preacher's yell was intended as a warning to Juanita just as much as a reproof for Damien Blake.

The burly teamster stood bolt upright, a snarl curling his lips as he whipped around to face Sorenson. Below him, Juanita stifled a little scream, then let out a most unladylike curse as she saw the towering figure of Blake silhouetted against the glowing pink of sunrise.

"Get the hell back to your prayers, Preacher!" Damien Blake raged as Sorenson advanced towards him.

"You're not to—to spy on that girl!" Sorenson blurted out.

"Yeah?" sneered Blake. "And since when have you been givin' orders around here, Preacher man? Get back to the camp! I'm gonna get better acquainted with this 'breed girl!"

"No!" Sorenson breathed, and stood his ground.

Below them, Juanita was hastily clambering out of the creek, the water gleaming on her skin as she groped for her clothes.

"Listen here, Preacher man," Damien Blake growled, "last night just about everyone, including you, was slaverin' around that 'breed, and I hardly got a look in. Well, I've decided to have my share—so like I said, get back to the wagons!"

Ignoring Sorenson, Blake began to blunder down the muddy bank, his heavy boots squelching in the mud. Juanita screamed as he came closer.

"Blake!" Abel Sorenson cried, clambering down the bank after him.

Blake whipped around as Sorenson grabbed at his thick arm to stop him. Surprise and fury registered on Damien Blake's face as the young preacher caught him off-balance, and with an oath, the teamster smashed an iron fist full into Sorenson's face. The missionary was plastered into the mud, blood spurting from his nose. Desperately, Sorenson scrambled to his feet, black mud smeared on his pants, and with an ugly grin, Blake measured him with his fists.

"No!" Juanita shrieked. "He's a preacher!"

"I don't give a damn what he is!" Damien Blake drove his first blow into the soft flesh just above Abel's belt. "I'm gonna preach him a sermon!"

Sorenson folded, wincing in pain as Blake's clenched fist thudded onto the back of his head. Gamely, the preacher lashed out with his fists, but only one blow connected, and Blake countered his onslaught with three knife-like punches to Abel's kidneys.

"Oh, God, no!" Juanita moaned. "He's not used to fighting! Stop—before you kill him!"

But Blake was enjoying himself. He thrust a knee into the preacher's belly, and as he jack-knifed, Blake slammed him in the neck. The preacher dropped face down in the soft mud.

Damien Blake stood triumphantly over him, a twisted smile on his lips.

"He's had enough, Blake!" Juanita wept, clutching her clothes to her body, but he thrust her aside.

"I haven't finished with him yet!"

Ruthlessly, Blake ground his boot into the back of Abel Sorenson's head, shoving his face deeper into the slush. Next he drove his other boot hard into the preacher's heaving ribs.

Moments later, an iron hand swung the teamster right around, and Shane Preston's knuckles blasted into his mouth like a hammer. Blake staggered back and Shane bored in. He landed a savage uppercut into the bully's jaw, jerking Blake's head back under the impact. Blake frantically tried to steady himself, but the gunfighter was relentless and even as the teamster swung at air, two fists ripped into the hardness of his chest. Gasping for breath, Blake waded forward, walking right into Shane's rock-hard knuckles. Blood spurted from Blake's mouth. He reeled, teetering on the brink of the water's edge. Hazily, he glimpsed Shane Preston charging at him, and seconds later the gunfighter's punch to his jaw lifted him clean off his feet and pitched him into the water.

Floundering and threshing, the burly bully fell down again as his boots slid on the slippery creek bed. Water was dripping off him as he crawled out of the creek to find a grinning audience watching from the bank. Shane was waiting for him. There was no amusement on the gunslinger's face, only cold anger, as he surveyed the drenched teamster emerging from the water.

"Hear this, Blake," he said. "Last night you made trouble, and now this! Next time you cut loose—I'll kill you."

The smiles went from the faces of the people of the wagon train. Damien Blake stood very still for a moment, then turned away and retched.

"I'm backing up what Shane did," called out Huss Whittaker. "Get back to your wagon, Blake."

Blake stared at him unseeingly, then blundered up the bank. Shane stood with Whittaker, watching him go.

"I don't like him any more than you do," Huston Whittaker grunted. "But the three of them in his wagon paid their dues like the others."

"Know something?" the tall gunfighter mused. "Blake told us he'd heard of gold west of Gun Creek, and that's where they'll be prospecting."

"So?"

"Jonah and I, we've lived in this territory for some time," Shane Preston remarked. "And we've never heard of gold anywhere near Gun Creek."

Whittaker frowned as the gunslinger marched ahead of him, back to the wagons.

"Sowing in the morning, sowing seeds of kindness,
   Sowing in the noontide, and the dewy eve:
   Waiting for the harvest, and the time of reaping,
   We shall come rejoicing, bringing in the sheaves!"

Shane Preston adjusted his steel shaving mirror and applied the sharp razor to his face as Sorenson's Sunday morning congregation sang a lusty hymn. He could see them beyond the tree to which he'd hooked his mirror. Standing beside the preacher, Brett Craig was providing musical accompaniment on his violin. Even old Jonah was there, singing with the rest of them.

"You're not a religious man, Shane?"

The gunfighter turned as Juanita came to perch on a boulder beside him.

"And evidently you aren't either, Juanita," he grinned.

"I was taught your religion at the Mission," Juanita recollected. "I even believed in it at the time."

"And now?" He shaved his chin.

"I've shocked Abel," she admitted. "In fact, he was so worried, he's spent the last two days on the trail trying to convert me. You see, I've reverted back to the religion of mother's people—belief in Wakonda."

"The Great Spirit?"

"Yes." She added: "I think Abel sees me as a challenge."

"I reckon he sees you as more than that," Shane Preston said dryly. "He's got that love-sick look in his eyes."

"But he keeps reminding me that I'm a runaway wife and he can't have anything to do with me," she told him.

Shane dashed cold water over his face, washing away the flecks of shaving soap. "Known a few preachers in my time," he stated. The congregation was launching into the gusty chorus of another hymn. "Some of them have been so damn self-righteous I've been glad I'm a sinner. Others have been men I could walk proud beside, along any street. I mightn't agree with all of Abel Sorenson's views, but he's one man I'd walk with."

"Me, too," Juanita whispered.

Shane put on his shirt and built a cigarette. The worshippers had sat down on wooden boxes and Abel was opening a big black Bible. Shane let his eyes wander past the congregation as the preacher read out the Old Testament lesson. The wagons were almost in the shadow of a low ridge which stretched across the prairie like a bald wall. It was a wind-swept ledge of rock and once Sorenson had pronounced the benediction, Shane would be leading the wagons over it. His eyes moved west along the ridge, and quite suddenly Shane froze.

There was a solitary pine reaching into the cloudless sky from the crest of the ridge, a lean, windblown tree etched against the sky like an arrowhead. And right beneath this pine was a lone rider.

"Shane!" Juanita had spotted the silent watcher, too, and her voice was edged with anxiety.

"A Cheyenne buck," Shane murmured, his eyes narrowing.

The rider was motionless. Sitting astride his pinto pony, he was a stark silhouette, naked from the waist up.

Jonah's gaze, straying away from the preacher reading the lesson, had found the rider, too, and the oldster nudged Huss Whittaker beside him. Soon a murmur was running through the assembly, and Janie Craig drew in her breath sharply. Perceiving that he'd lost the attention of his congregation, Abel Sorenson glanced up from the Old Testament and stared at the ridge at which everyone else was looking.

Shane stepped swiftly up to the preacher's side.

Craig had thrust his violin away, and his right hand was groping for his gun.

"No!" Shane's restraining command was like a whip-crack in the silence.

"But, heck—that's an Indian, a red savage!" Brett Craig croaked.

"One of those Cheyenne renegades, I'll be bound!" Whittaker blurted out.

"And he'll be a scout," Shane informed them. "If we kill him, the shot'll bring a war-party right this way."

"What can we do?" Janie Craig wailed, clutching her little daughter to her skirts.

"Right now we'll carry on with the church service," the gunfighter commanded. "If those redskins from the Reservation are out there and meaning to attack us, they'll come anyway. If that rider's just a stray buck, and harmless, we're worrying about nothing. The main thing is to act normal but keep your hardware handy—and that means the womenfolk, too. Keep a gun by you at all times."

"And after church?" Craig asked.

"We pull on out," Shane said. "We should reach Gaucho late this afternoon, and we'll just keep going till we make the town. And remember what I said about guns, but no shooting unless I give the word. There's no telling that those Cheyennes will attack, and we sure don't want to provoke an incident."

"I must confess," Abel Sorenson said, "that I don't possess a gun."

"Jonah carries a couple of spares." Shane nodded to his pard sitting with a hymn sheet on his lap. "That is, Abel, if it ain't against your beliefs to shoot a man?"

Sorenson swallowed. "The Good Book does say an eye for an eye, Shane."

"Yeah," Shane said, his eyes still on the lone rider.

"But then," Sorenson soliloquized, "I am a man of the cloth!"

"Jonah will give you a gun," Shane said gently. "Whether you use it or not is up to you, Preacher."

The Indian moved, edging his pony slowly along the ridge.

As if hypnotized, the pioneers watched the lean figure, and when he turned his head, they glimpsed the long black hair held back by a red band.

"Abel," Shane said, "you haven't finished the lesson."

Sorenson continued reading, his voice quavering a little in the silence. Shane stepped to one side, his eyes focused on the lone scout. The preacher announced a hymn, and Craig struck up a half-hearted tune. Shane glanced at the grim-faced wagoners as they rose to their feet to sing, then he looked back at the ridge.

It was empty.

The rider had vanished and now only the solitary pine thrust up from the bare ridge. Right then, a cloud obscured the sun and the prairie was blotted out as if by a dark tide. A moaning wind seemed to spring up from nowhere, providing an eerie accompaniment of the strains of the violin. And the emigrants huddled together to sing the hymn in the middle of the wilderness.

·

FOUR

LAWMAN OF GAUCHO

Gaucho seemed to jump up out of the prairie. One moment the wagons were swaying through the whispering grass, the next moment they spilled out of the yellow sea to the mouth of a small valley.

Whittaker spurred his mount to where Shane and Jonah sat saddle, surveying the prairie community below them. Gaucho had once been a fort, and when the military abandoned it in favor of Fort Defiance, settlers moved inside its walls and built their homes inside the stockade. Now the town had spread beyond the walls, and rows of adobe houses were built along a crudely paved street.

"Remember the last time we stopped off here for the night?" the elder gun hawk grinned broadly.

"Seem to recall that the sheriff didn't take too kindly to our presence," Shane Preston said dryly.

"He wouldn't be the only lawman to take that unreasonable attitude," Jonah quipped.

"From the way you two talk, you ain't exactly in the good books with the territory's badge-toters," Huss Whittaker remarked.

"We're gunfighters, Huss," Shane reminded him tersely. "I reckon that just about sums it up."

The wagons had ground to a halt, and now the emigrants were either riding or walking towards the crest. They gathered around the wagon master.

"We pull out at sundown," Whittaker said. "Which gives us about two hours in Gaucho for buying supplies and such."

The emigrants needed no second prompting. Leaving their wagons, they streamed down the slope, each one wanting to be the first to enter this oasis in the wilderness. The towners had seen them coming, and folks gathered in groups on the main street to await the pioneers. Traders, looking forward to a bonanza, hastily marked a few prices up and opened their doors wider. Within minutes, the emigrants were flocking along the street, exchanging greetings with the towners of Gaucho, who made them more than welcome, it wasn't often that this community had visitors.

Shane and Jonah made straight for the town's only saloon, the Faro Wheel, and strode up to the bar.

"Name it, gents," the bartender said cheerfully.

"Rye," Shane said.

The Faro Wheel was almost deserted. In fact, the only patrons sat hunched around a table playing cards, while a good-time girl who looked like she'd seen better days hovered over them like an elderly hawk.

"Heard of any Cheyenne trouble?" Shane Preston asked the lanky bartender.

"Not exactly trouble," the man replied guardedly. "But there's Indian signs all over the prairie."

Shane sipped his rye.

"Last night, Sam Napier checked his game-traps beyond the ridge where your wagons are," the saloon man said. "A couple of Injun bucks had raided the traps, and Sam saw them sneakin' off."

"Did he plug them?" Jonah Jones asked.

"Hell, no!" the bartender exploded. "Gaucho's a long ways from Fort Defiance, mister, and if those Cheyennes got riled, they'd take this town apart. Same goes for your wagon train, too."

Shane downed his drink and reached for the bottle.

"There's a story goin' around, 'bout this bunch of renegades," the bartender informed them. "Ole Mert Sinclair passed through a week ago."

"That old mountain goat!" Jonah grinned widely.

"He's still a travellin' salesman," the bartender rejoined. "Seems he was visited by a coupla Cheyennes just out from Milly's Well."

"Hell!" Jonah ejaculated. "Has Mert still got his hair?"

"They came to trade," the bartender said. "He ended up selling them some blankets and tobacco, but here's the funny bit. They paid him in gold."

"Gold!" Jonah gaped.

"He showed me the nuggets himself," the bartender recalled. "Big chunks of yellow rock!"

"But—but where in the hell would those redskins get gold from?" the old-timer frowned.

"He asked them that same question," the barkeep shrugged. "They claimed they dug them out of the dry creek on their Reservation. And there's more to the story. Ole Mert claims they showed him a whole bag full of the damn rocks."

"So those pesky red varmints are ridin' around totin' a fortune?"

"Seems so," the saloon man said. "And it's got the army worried. After all, if the renegades have gold, that means they could buy rifles."

"But you wouldn't find many white men who'd sell guns to Indians, specially a renegade bunch," Jonah said.

"Not too many, Jonah," Shane Preston agreed. "But there's always the man who doesn't give a damn about the consequences so long as he gets rich."

It was a sobering thought, and one which made the old-timer gulp down his drink and build a cigarette.

Right then, the gunfighters heard the thud of boots on the creaky wooden boardwalk outside. The batwings lurched open and the white-faced figure of Janie Craig stood in the saloon entrance. Unsure of herself in this man's province, she glanced around timidly at the bottles of liquor, the garish posters on the walls and the hag-like saloon woman who faced her with arms folded over her spilling breasts. Then Janie's eyes found the men she'd been looking for.

"Oh, please," she cried to Shane and Jonah. "Come quickly!"

Shane dumped his glass down on the bar counter, and with Jonah close, the tall gunfighter loped across the sawdust.

"Shane," the emigrant woman said frantically, "something terrible's happened. My Brett's been arrested!"

"By the damn sheriff of this town?" Jonah snapped.

"He was waiting for him." Janie started to cry. "We—we headed into the general store, and the lawman was there ready with his gun to arrest him. I—I came to you because Brett said that—that you were on his side, Shane!"

"Where's Brett now?" demanded Shane.

"I ran straight over here," Janie breathed. "He's probably still in the general store with that sheriff."

"Right now he's coming up the street with a gun in his back," Jonah Jones grated, peering over the batwings.

"Janie," the lean gun hawk murmured, "go to your kids and leave this to us."

Shane stepped out onto the boardwalk.

A crowd was gathering on the street, towners and emigrants all watching as Brett Craig trod the dust with his hands high. Behind him, swaggering and grinning, walked Sheriff Wayne Vandermann, his gun poking into Craig's spine. The prisoner glanced helplessly around him as Vandermann shoved him towards the Spanish-arched door of his law office.

Shane didn't run. He headed slowly and deliberately in the direction of the door.

Suddenly, Sheriff Vandermann's eyes narrowed and his guttural curse halted Brett Craig in his tracks.

"Preston!" Sheriff Vandermann blinked. "What in hell are *you* doing here?"

"Now, Sheriff, what sort of a welcome is that?" Shane chided him, leaning against the wall of the law office.

"The welcome you damn well deserve!" Vandermann blurted out.

"Fact is, Sheriff," Shane said, "me and Jonah are scouts for this outfit."

"Scouts!" Vandermann echoed scornfully. "Since when have you two polecats earned your keep other than by gunslinging?"

The crowd listened in silence, thronging the boardwalks to watch. Whittaker was holding onto one of Brett Craig's children, a little lad who was sobbing violently.

"Anyhow, Preston," Vandermann growled, "right now you don't bother me none. I've other things on my mind."

"Like taking in an innocent man?"

Vandermann stared at the gunfighter. Gaucho's sheriff was a thickset lawman with a middle-aged spread that folded over his belt. Almost bald, Vandermann's big, bullet head showed a sparse growth of hair.

"Once a month, Preston," Sheriff Vandermann stated slowly, "this town gets its mail, and in the last drop, I got a reward dodger on Brett Craig. In the same dispatch was a message givin' me a tip-off from a fellow-lawman that Craig was on this wagon train. Seems this outlaw was figuring that Gun Creek was far enough away from the scene of his crime, and the law wouldn't bother to chase him there. And Craig's probably right. That's why I'm grabbin' him now, before he gets to Gun Creek. Any objection to an elected lawman doing his duty, Preston?"

"Sheriff!" Brett Craig croaked. "Sure I killed Tramner, but it was a fair fight! I'm only on the run because Tramner had friends—powerful friends!"

Vandermann shrugged callously. "Tell it to the judge. Craig."

"A judge back in Tombstone?" cried Craig. "With a jury loaded with Tramner's old friends?"

Shane had moved to stand directly in front of the law office door.

"Any objection to me doing my duty, Preston?" Sheriff Vandermann repeated.

"Right now—yes," Shane said bluntly.

Vandermann smirked at him. "I'm real surprised at you, Preston. I know you ain't exactly loved by us badge-toters, but you've always managed to stay inside the law. Hinderin' a sheriff in the course of his duty happens to be a felony."

"I'm not hindering you, Vandermann." Shane heard the gasps from the onlookers as he slipped the gun from his holster and weighed it in the palm of his hand. "I'm just objecting to you grabbing my prisoner."

"Huh?" Vandermann was nonplussed.

"You heard me, Sheriff," Shane murmured, his left hand stroking the gleaming steel of his six-shooter. "My prisoner."

"But—hell!"

"You asked me what we were doing here, and I said we were scouts for this wagon train. Reckon that's only partly true."

Vandermann looked around him, bewildered and frowning. Just along the boardwalk, old Jonah was squatting on his heels, and the pudgy gunslinger's six-shooter was resting casually in his hands.

"Fact is, we're on two jobs," Shane Preston said. "In addition to being scouts, we're taking Craig in for the bounty money on his head. We joined the wagon train so we could grab him."

Sheer disbelief clouded the lawman's face, then a sneer curled his lips.

"Craig your prisoner?" demanded the sheriff. "And you let him walk loose in the streets of town?"

"Why not?" Shane shrugged. "There's no place he could go. Gaucho's a town plumb in the center of the wilderness. A man would be loco to try to cross the prairie on his ownsome, with Cheyennes skulking around."

Vandermann gave his prisoner a shove with his gun muzzle, moving him right to the very edge of the boardwalk. Still Shane stayed by the door.

"Well, Preston," Sheriff Vandermann grinned for the benefit of the onlooking towners. "Thanks very much for holding this prisoner until now. I'll be taking him into custody and I'll see that you get the reward bounty."

"Too bad, Sheriff." Shane Preston leveled his six-shooter. "That ain't convenient to us."

"What're you sayin'?" fumed Vandermann.

"It ain't that we don't trust you, Sheriff," Shane said politely. "But it so happens we promised Dan

74

Hogan we'd take him back to the County Seat so he can stand trial there."

"Hogan?" Vandermann stared at Shane. *"Hogan sent you?"*

"Well," Shane drawled, "there's no way you can check it out, so you'll just have to take my word for it. We're taking Craig with us while we guide these settlers to Gun Creek, then we're cutting north straight for the County Seat to deliver this outlaw and collect our bounty money. Right, Jonah?"

"Right," beamed Jonah Jones.

Vandermann glanced around him. It was like he was on trial. He could see that the emigrants didn't want to leave one of their number in his jail, but the towners were waiting for a show of strength from the man they'd appointed to wear the badge. Vandermann stood on the brink. Suddenly his face hardened.

"You're a coupla liars!" he accused Shane and Jonah. Then he jabbed the prisoner with his gun. "Keep walking right into the law office."

"Vandermann!" The tone of Shane Preston's voice told everyone that the time for talking was over. He thumbed back the hammer of his six-shooter. *"I'm taking back my prisoner."*

The lawman froze.

Jonah eased his stocky frame upright and leveled his gun.

Vandermann's eyes darted around at the onlookers for a sign of support from the people of Gaucho. But no one moved, not one hand even crept gun-wards. There wasn't a single towner who'd take his chances against the two fastest guns in the State. Sweat beaded Sheriff Vandermann's brow. Cold sweat.

"All right," the badge-toter backed down, his voice quivering with anger. "Take your prisoner, Preston. And keep him close—or by God, you'll answer for it."

"Craig," Shane said quietly, "get back to your wagon."

"Sure, Mr. Preston," the outlaw said respectfully.

Sheriff Vandermann's face was grim as Brett Craig sauntered away. The lawman stared at the gunfighter leaning against his door, and then he mounted the boardwalk. There was a half smile on Shane's face as he stood aside for the fuming badge-toter.

"One helluva law-abidin' wagon train, I must say!" The lawman's sarcasm was directed at the emigrants as well as Shane Preston. "Two gunslingers, one outlaw, and one hombre just out of the damn penitentiary!"

"What do you mean?" Shane demanded.

"Do I have to spell it out for you?" Sheriff Vandermann laughed. "First there's you and that bearded ole coot—"

"Who's just out of the penitentiary?" insisted Shane Preston.

76

"You mean you don't know?" the law officer snickered. "Damien Blake!"

Whittaker had detached himself from the crowd and joined Shane on the boardwalk.

"Saw Blake a few minutes ago up the street," Vandermann recounted. "First time I've seen him since Tonto Rim—that's where I was deputy to Sheriff Anderson ten years ago. I remember the night they brought Blake in, caught red-handed rustlin' beeves from the Circle K. Anderson arranged a real quick trial and Blake was sentenced to ten years behind bars. Unless he was sprung earlier for good behavior, I reckon he's just been released."

Shane digested this piece of information as he holstered his gun.

"Next time I'm passing through I'll buy you a drink," the tall gunslinger told him.

"Don't bother!" Sheriff Vandermann grated, storming inside and slamming the door.

"Shane," Huss Whittaker's face was creased with concern. "What the hell's going on? First Craig, now Blake—what sorta wagon train have we got?"

"Ride back to the wagons with me, Huss," Shane told the bewildered wagon master. "On the way, we'll have a talk about both those hombres."

Shane paced across the street to where Snowfire was tethered at the tie-rail. Scratching his head, the wagon master trailed along behind him.

Shane swung into the saddle, and moments later he was heading back up the street to the prairie trail.

Jonah joined Shane and the wagon master, and the trio walked their horses towards the crest.

"Figured that was real interestin'—the way you brought in Sheriff Hogan's name," Jonah Jones quipped.

"Yeah, real interesting," Shane drawled. "'Specially since I've never met Hogan in my life!"

"Move 'em out!"

Whittaker's raucous command rang out over the prairie and the wagons began to creak and sway into the sunset.

Whips cracked, steers bawled, horses snorted as the wagon train moved farther away from civilization into the wide prairie country. Sundown was a vivid blood-red streak across the distant ridges as Shane and Jonah rode ahead of the first ponderous wagon. For one full hour, the emigrants pressed farther along the trail, but after the dark hand of night enclosed them, Shane called a halt.

The nightly ritual of making the wagons into a circle was soon accomplished, and Shane sat just beyond the camp to keep watch as preparations were made for the evening meal. The gunfighter smoked alone, his keen eyes staring out into the night. Beyond the camp, night owls called to each other and the prairie scavengers, the coyotes, padded around in hunting packs. It was in situations like this, when he was alone, that memories would flood back. Memories of a happy wife, slim, dark-haired, incredibly beautiful in his eyes. He remembered her musical voice, the way she'd come out and help him on the range, the times they spent together out riding, the soft warmth of her young body in his bed. Then he saw that bloodied, lifeless heap on the floor, the woman he loved murdered by two thieves, and once again he was trailing them to that border saloon. Coldness came over him as he recalled shooting the fat outlaw before Scarface blasted a slug into his belly. Scarface, the last of the two killers, the man he had to find!

"Preston!"

"What is it, Blake?" Shane asked, without turning his head.

Damien Blake drew deeply on his cigarette. "The roster says it's my turn to stand guard."

Shane slid off the boulder and faced the beefy teamster.

"Okay," the gunfighter said, "I'll leave you to it."

"Before you go—" Blake said harshly. "There's something I want to say to you."

"I'm listening," Shane said in the silence.

"Some of the folks heard what that fool lawman said about me," Damien Blake growled.

"About you being in the pen?"

79

"What he said was true," Blake admitted grudgingly. "Once I was a rustler. Maybe I even took more beeves than those from the Circle K! But that was ten years ago, and I served my time. I paid the penalty, Preston."

"And now you're a decent, God-fearing citizen?" Shane Preston was unable to conceal the mockery in his voice.

"Yeah." Blake's face darkened. "That's exactly what I am, Preston!"

Shane contemplated the teamster with cold eyes.

"There's something I've been meaning to ask you, Blake," the gun hawk said.

"Ask away," Damien Blake invited, squatting on the boulder.

"Did you hear anything the night Jim Cutting was knifed?"

Blake glanced sharply at him, and there was a long moment before he replied, "Nothing."

"He was knifed right beside your wagon, yet you heard nothing?"

"That's what I said."

"You know, Blake," the gunfighter murmured. "There's a story going around that you and Cutting didn't exactly see eye to eye."

"Who told you that?"

"Did you and Cutting quarrel?" Shane insisted.

"Preston," Damien Blake growled, "chow's ready back in the camp."

Shane studied him for a moment, then he headed away towards the wagons. He passed the prospectors' wagon and Eli McKay watched him from the front seat. He strode to the roaring fire where Juanita shoved a plate into his hands.

"Soup, Shane?" she asked him. "I made it myself."

FIVE

RENDEZVOUS WITH MURDER!

"How much longer?" Preacher Sorenson leaned forward in the wagon seat as Shane rode past and signaled towards the hollow in the prairie just ahead. "When shall we see Gun Creek?"

"Two days' ride, maybe three," Shane called up to him out of the swirling dust. "But right now we're stopping for the night."

Seated beside Sorenson, Juanita let her gaze lift to the ranges. All day, the ridges and the crags had loomed closer, and as the afternoon had progressed, patches of pumice had littered the sun bleached prairie. Tomorrow, they would climb, groping up the last stretch before they reached the walls of Fort Defiance.

Shane rode back along the wagon line, and Sorenson turned his team into the hollow. Suddenly the front wheel rim struck a sharp rock and the wagon lurched drunkenly. Juanita was thrown violently against the preacher, and instinctively, Abel Sorenson clasped an arm around her to prevent her from toppling over. The swaying stopped but the emigrant still held the girl in the crook of his arm, and Juanita made no effort to draw away from him. The young preacher trembled as he felt her softness nestling against his body, and all at once he thrust her gently away. Red-faced, he picked up the reins and flicked them over his team.

Dusk was closing in like a gray blanket as the wagoners once again made camp. It was colder that night, and they were glad of the big fire that Jonah Jones soon lit for them. The 'breed girl busied herself preparing supper and Brett Craig took first watch. As always when her husband was standing guard beyond the wagons, Janie Craig found difficulty in controlling all three of her children. She managed to thrust a plate of food in front of her daughter and youngest son, but Pete, the eldest, had somehow sneaked away.

The six-year-old lad made straight for the make-shift corral the men always made to pen the animals for the night. Pete's young eyes searched the dusty square enclosed by the wooden stakes and crosslines until they found the black and white goat which was his pet. A grin came over Pete's freckled features as Samantha scampered over to him. For a while, Pete stroked the she-goat's head, then he tired of this and began to wander back towards the wagons. He swung on a wagon wheel, peering through the wooden spokes at the fire where his mother was anxiously scanning the darkness for him. Knowing full well that Juanita and the other women had cooked vegetable stew for supper, Pete elected to stay away a little longer.

The boy slipped under a wagon and lay in the grass. It was then that he realized whose wagon he was under—Blake's. Pete had explored every wagon, even the preacher's, except the one lived in by those three gold prospectors. Always Blake's wagon was closed up. Both the front and rear entrances through the canvas were usually lashed up with rawhide, but tonight Pete's curiosity was reaching a peak now he actually lay under the only wagon left unexplored.

On an impulse, Pete slithered out from beneath the wagon and climbed up the back steps. The lashed-up flap presented a challenge. Nimble fingers began to untie the rope, threading it out through the holes. Just beyond him, standing around the fire lit circle, were the wagoners. Tentatively, Pete peered inside the wagon, seeing only darkness. He edged a hand inside and touched solid wood. It felt hard and cold, like the boxes that held the preacher's books. He poked his head inside.

Suddenly, an iron hand grabbed him by the scruff of his neck. Pete screamed as he was swiveled around and brought face to face with the angry, bulging eyes of Damien Blake. The teamster's fist slapped Pete's left ear, knocking him clean off the steps and into the grass. Weeping, the boy tried to clamber up. Blake was uncoiling a short bullwhip. The folks around the fire stared in amazement and horror as Blake cracked the whip ruthlessly around Pete Craig's legs.

"That'll teach you to trespass in my wagon, kid!" Blake grated, his eyes glowing insanely.

Sobbing, Pete crawled away in the grass. Janie gathered up her skirts and raced towards the beefy teamster as he trod relentlessly after the boy.

Pete screamed hysterically as the whip swished like a snake in the moonlight.

"Blasted nosy kid!" stormed Blake, standing over him now. "If you come near my wagon again, I'll thrash the hide off you!"

Janie plunged past Blake, throwing herself over her son to protect him with her body. Muttering, the teamster stepped back. Reb Morton was already rethreading the rawhide at the flap as Blake stood there with his chest heaving.

"Blake!" The harsh challenge came from across the other side of the camp.

Damien Blake turned to face the man who had just come in from standing watch. Drawn by the commotion, Brett Craig had loped back, and now he stood with his right hand hovering over his gun holster.

"Your kid was trespassin', Craig," Blake rapped. "Pokin' his damn nose where he shouldn't!"

"You filthy bully!" Brett Craig erupted. "A kid of six happens to climb into your wagon and you whip him like he's a grown-up thief!"

"This wagon's private property," snarled Blake. "We've valuable things inside—the kid could have broken somethin' real important."

"Like what?" Huss Whittaker demanded, advancing from the fire.

"Minin' instruments," Eli McKay spoke up quickly. "Real intricate ones that a kid wandering around could easy break. Now I don't go along with Damien whippin' the lad, but we don't want kids nosing around where they might do costly harm."

"You whipped my boy, Blake," Brett Craig snapped. "Now I'm gonna give you the chance to face up to someone your own size. You've got a gun—make your play!"

Blake stared at him. Janie took hold of Pete's arm and dragged him clear.

"Wait!" Shane Preston paced between them. "There'll be no gunplay!"

"That bastard attacked my kid!" Craig exploded.

"Listen—both of you," Shane said harshly. "All of you listen! This is no time for us to go killing each other, whatever the reason! The Cheyennes are out there somewhere, and although we've been lucky up to now, there's no saying we won't get attacked before we make Fort Defiance. And if that happens, we'll need every man and woman on this wagon train able and ready to fire a gun. This is no time for us to be burying either one of you two."

"Hell, Shane—" Brett Craig was still fuming.

"Blake," Shane turned to the beefy teamster. "I reckon you owe Craig and his lad an apology."

Damien Blake looked like he was going to explode again, and he glanced first at Shane, then at Brett Craig. The big teamster's hand was inches from his gun, but slowly he drew it away.

"Damien," Eli McKay urged him softly.

"It won't happen again," Blake relented, and stalked off into the darkness.

Jonah edged up to his taller companion.

"Seems like Blake's real touchy about anyone bein' close to his wagon," the oldster mumbled. "Yesterday he chawed my ear just fer sittin' on his wagon steps to roll a cigarette!"

Shane ate his food, his eyes on the rear flap of the Blake wagon. Morton had just finished rethreading the rawhide and was tying the rope-ends into a knot.

"Yeah," Shane said thoughtfully, "real touchy."

It was past midnight, and the fire had burned low. Just a few hours before, the flames had been leaping over the logs, but now all that remained were glowing embers fanned by the chill prairie wind. The dying fire still threw out a vague semblance of warmth, but it was a warmth that didn't reach the lonely man hunched on the far side of the hollow.

Huston Whittaker's vigil was almost over. In just a half hour, Shane would come out of the camp to replace him, and the gunfighter would remain on guard until the grayness of dawn showed above the eastern plateau.

Now Whittaker rubbed his hands together. He had considered walking back to camp for a sip of whisky to warm his belly, but thought better of it. The lives of a lot of sleeping people were entrusted to his vigilance, and his senses had to be completely alert. Anyhow, in just a few minutes Shane would take over and he could return to his wagon bed and doze beside his sleeping wife.

It was the cracking of a twig that startled him.

Instinctively, Huston Whittaker dropped a hand to the cold steel of his Winchester. He stood up in the darkness. He heard another sharp snap coming from the other side of the hollow. Maybe it was some animal prowling. Nevertheless, he was on guard, and the sound had to be investigated. He began to circle the sides of the hollow, passing the silent wagons. He gripped his gun as he paused and searched the night. All he could hear was the eerie moan of the wind.

Treading softly, he glided right around the other side of the camp. Standing there beside a clump of brush, he listened intently. Apart from the wind, he heard nothing. He was about to walk back to his station when some sixth sense made him look up.

Whittaker froze as he glimpsed the moving figure, a dark silhouette against the moon. The man was right on the crest of the hollow, and Huston Whittaker's eyes watched him as he ran swiftly along the rim, finally to vanish into the darkness.

The wagon master clambered up the side of the hollow. He clawed at the long grass to lever himself higher, and breathing heavily, he climbed to the crest. Below him, the wagon camp was sleeping. Beyond stretched the prairie, dark and mysterious under the jeweled void.

Whittaker glanced around him, then made for the place where the figure had disappeared. Pausing, the emigrant looked hard into the grass until his eyes found a spot where the dry stalks had been flattened. Whittaker edged to the trail that had been made into the prairie, and with his rifle poised, he pushed his way into the grass.

Suddenly, out here, away from the camp, he felt very much alone. He stole a quick glance over his shoulder before he inched carefully along the trail of flattened grass.

He dropped as the sound of low voices came to him.

Just ahead, framed in the ghostly moonlight, were three figures. One was Eli McKay, and he was talking in soft tones and gesticulating with two men who were sitting astride ponies. Shaking, Whittaker eased his shoulders up, and peered over the top of the grass.

A terrible coldness lanced through him as he glimpsed the bronze faces and aquiline noses of McKay's companions. The riders were naked above the waist, lean and bony, and long, raven hair splashed down over their shoulders.

"Where's Vittorio?" he heard McKay ask.

The tallest Indian looked down at the teamster. For a moment, he said nothing. Then:

"Vittorio come soon," the Cheyenne buck stated in a harsh, guttural tone.

McKay moved right up to the tall brave's horse.

"And the gold?" the white man snapped.

Concealed in the grass, Huss Whittaker heard the second Indian laugh softly.

"It is here," the Indian said.

"Where?" McKay insisted.

"Vittorio will hand over the gold when the white-eyes give us what we want."

"You'll have them sure enough," McKay assured them. "We haven't come all this way for nothin'! We've brought a whole damn wagon-load of rifles, enough to make Vittorio and all of you happy."

Frozen with horror, Whittaker saw the tall Indian slide like a snake from his pony.

"And ammunition?" the savage wanted to know.

McKay replied, "Enough to last you all for one helluva long time—more than a year."

"Where is Blake?" The tall Cheyenne changed the subject abruptly.

"He'll be here soon."

"That is good," the redskin nodded. "Vittorio arranged this with Blake—he wants him here."

Anger was pulsing through Whittaker now. He'd been fooled into believing that Blake and his two companions were genuine settlers, prospectors on the way west to prospect for gold. Well, there was gold waiting for them, all right, gold in exchange for running rifles to these renegades! This was obviously a prearranged rendezvous and Blake had been using the wagon train as a cover to run his dangerous cargo to the Cheyennes. Now Whittaker understood why Damien Blake had treated Pete Craig so brutally for poking a head into his wagon. Holding his breath, Whittaker decided to crawl backwards through the grass. The emigrants had to be alerted and this vile trade prevented. Like all frontiersmen,

Huss Whittaker knew the terrible cost in lives and property when Indians with rifles went on a rampage.

He edged backwards, hearing McKay laugh as he tried to show one of the Indians how to roll a cigarette.

All at once the wagon master saw a booted foot inches from his face.

Filled with a terrible fear, he screwed his head sideways and squinted up. Damien Blake was straddling him and his gun was leveled at Whittaker's head.

"Get up!" Blake snarled.

Damien Blake's voice carried to McKay and the two Indians, and their faces whipped around in the night.

"I've met lowdown buzzards in my time, Blake," said Whittaker as he propped himself up on his arms. "But lousy gunrunners beat them all!"

"Quit the sermon and get up!"

Reb Morton was standing right behind Blake.

"And leave that gun in the grass!"

McKay and the two Cheyennes were approaching as Huston Whittaker gradually eased his frame out of the prairie grass and stood up. The wind ruffled his hair as he faced the gunrunners. They ringed him, white men and Indians, five of them, and it was the loneliest moment of his life.

"Whittaker," Blake's voice was hoarse. "Start walkin'!"

Morton fingered the handle of his knife, and a grim smile played over his lips.

Whittaker hesitated.

"Walk!" Blake said bleakly.

"What's it to be, Blake?" the wagon master asked. "In the back—the way Jim Cutting got it!"

"Cutting was a nosy, interferin' fool," snarled Damien Blake.

In desperation, Huss Whittaker plunged between the two pinto ponies, and started running into the prairie. Blake's urgent cry rang out as one of the ponies reared and Whittaker raced on. The wagon master waded through the waist-high grass, blazing a path with his frantic legs. There was a long, terrible silence, then Huss Whittaker felt a hot shaft sink into the center of his back. Glassy-eyed, the wagon master sank to his knees, and like hounds coming in for the kill, the men closed in. But Whittaker could not see their faces, because as they stood around him, his eyelids closed like doors and he fell into that bottomless pit called death.

SIX

THE PARTING OF THE TRAIL

Shane Preston headed out to where he knew Whittaker should be waiting for him. He strode past the preacher's wagon, noting with a grin that Juanita was huddled beneath her saddle blanket right beside his wooden steps. As yet she hadn't made it to the interior of Sorenson's canvas-covered wagon, but Shane reminded himself that there were still a couple of nights left before they reached the fort.

The gunfighter strode out of the wagon circle and mounted the slope. He halted and frowned as he saw the place where Whittaker usually sat, but couldn't make out the wagon master's figure.

He stalked over and stood there, his keen eyes scanning the night. The wind mocked him.

"Huss!" Shane called softly, figuring that maybe the wagon master had taken a walk around the other side of the camp. "Huss—I've come to relieve you!"

His only answer was the moaning breeze.

"Huss!" Shane's voice was urgent now.

The gunfighter's eyes searched the slope, focusing on the beaten grass leading around the circumference of the hollow. Shane dropped a hand to his black six-shooter and drew it out. He began to follow the boot prints, heading around to the far side of the camp. Shane paused as he glimpsed the trail nosing up to the crest. Thumbing back his gun hammer, Shane climbed the slope and padded along the crest to where the trail plunged into the prairie.

Cautiously, the gunfighter headed into the grass.

An owl hooted somewhere in the darkness. Shane Preston knew at once that it was a human owl.

Moving like a panther, he came upon a big patch of trampled grass, and as the hooting sounded ghost-like in the night, he glimpsed the prints of unshod hooves.

His eyes followed another trail through the grass, leading away from the flattened patch, and swiftly he trod his way down it. The tracks ended abruptly where blood was spattered over broken stalks of grass.

Shane knelt down and ran his fingers over the dark smears of sticky wetness.

He stood up and retraced his footsteps to the flat patch.

It was then that he saw the wide trail made by more than one pair of boots cutting back to the crest. Clutching his gun, he headed along the trail. A shadowy rider moved to his left, seemingly gliding through the whispering grass. Shane leveled his six-shooter, but before he could take aim, the specter melted into the void. He heard distant hooting, followed by silence.

Shane ran back to the crest, stopping where the tracks veered along the rim before dropping sharply down the slope. He headed to the place where the trail moved away at a tangent, his eyes slitting as he saw how the tracks twisted towards Blake's wagon. The gunfighter climbed down the slope, edging through the thick grass just beyond the long canvas-topped schooner where Blake's crew slept. He crouched down and let his eyes wander over the length of the wagon and finally drop to the steps.

Shane studied the wagon for a long moment, then began to creep towards the front end. The lean gun hawk levered himself up into the driving seat. Something terrible and sinister had happened to Huss Whittaker, and Shane figured that the answer lay in this wagon.

Slowly, he started to unthread the rawhide that held the flap in place.

He pulled out the rope and inched the flap aside.

The interior of the wagon was enclosed in darkness.

"Preston!" The soft voice came from behind him. "Toss down your gun or I'll blow a hole right through the back of your head!"

Shane stood up on the wagon seat, freezing as he heard a rustle in the grass.

"Now!" snarled the voice.

Shane Preston slowly opened his fingers, and his notched six-shooter slithered down, bounced on the wagon seat, and spun away to drop into the clay.

"Where's Whittaker?" Shane demanded as the beefy teamster emerged from the grass.

The interior of the wagon seemed to spring to life. A long rifle protruded between two huge crates, and Shane glimpsed the stubbled chin of Reb Morton. A shadow moved from behind another crate, and McKay cocked his six-shooter as he scrambled forward over the wagon floor.

"As you see, Preston," Blake smiled softly. "Me and the boys have been waitin' for you. When we saw you moseying off out there, we figured you'd find our trail back here and come and start nosin' around."

"Whittaker!" Shane repeated.

McKay grinned mockingly. "Well now, Whittaker happened to find out a few things just a mite before time, so we—ah—had to kill him. Ended up like Jim Cutting, you might say."

"You bastards!" Shane Preston whispered, as he pictured his friend with a knife in his back.

"You see, Preston," Damien Blake said casually, "Whittaker overheard Eli here arranging with a couple of our Cheyenne friends how we're going to hand over our wagon load of rifles in exchange for their gold."

Shane's burning eyes stared incredulously at the gunrunner. A terrible, boiling anger began to simmer inside of him as the full impact of Blake's cool, calculated statement struck him.

"Might as well tell you everythin' now," Blake shrugged. "After all, it won't matter since you'll all be buzzard-bait in just a real short time."

"What sort of men are you?" Shane Preston accused, his cold eyes moving from one to the other.

"Businessmen, Preston," Blake said simply. "All three of us are businessmen selling our goods to the highest bidder, which in this case happens to be the Cheyennes. Chief Vittorio's paying us with gold, real yellow nuggets."

"And after these customers of yours get their rifles?" the gunfighter pressed him. "What if they go on a rampage, killing white folks?"

"I don't give a damn," Blake replied bluntly. The beefy gunrunner motioned to his two companions. "Okay—you both know what you have to do."

Morton and McKay clambered past the gunfighter and jumped down to the ground.

"Don't worry, Preston," Damien Blake said, "they're only going to wake the folks up. You see, we're aimin' to disarm 'em and herd 'em all together so no damn fool starts shootin' at us when we pull our wagon out."

"And when's that to be?" Shane demanded.

"In just a coupla minutes," Blake told him. "The Cheyennes are out there waiting for us. Everything's worked pretty well for us up till now, Preston. In fact, it was a damn good notion—taking a wagonful of rifles on an emigrant train! The army have been on the look-out for gunrunners, but who'd suspect three gold-seekers travelin' west on a wagon train?"

Shane glanced inside the wagon. With all in readiness for the trade with the Indians, the attempts at concealment had been cast aside. Long crates were exposed where canvas covers had been pulled away, and Shane calculated that the wagon carried enough rifles to supply a full-scale Indian uprising.

The gunfighter looked back at the camp.

Reb Morton's rifle had just been jabbed into Juanita's ribs, and the 'breed girl awoke with a start. Bewildered, she obeyed the gunrunner's command to get up and walk over to the charred remains of the campfire.

Next, Abel Sorenson walked sleepily across the ground, an incongruous figure in his long nightshirt. The preacher's white hands were held high. Old Jonah stirred and Shane had to watch helplessly as

99

McKay's rifle muzzle jabbed into his partner's head. The pudgy gun hawk mouthed a curse and groped his way out of his blankets. Rubbing his red eyes, Jonah stood beside Juanita and the preacher as Reb Morton herded the Craig family out of their wagon. Carrying their crying kids, Brett and Janie Craig were shoved towards the others. Last of all, Gloria Whittaker was awakened, and the woman burst into tears as McKay coldly informed her that she was a widow. Soon all the emigrants stood in a frightened huddle, the children sobbing at this rude awakening from their night's rest.

"Join them, Preston," Damien Blake commanded.

The tall gunfighter climbed down, and with Blake's gun in his back, he headed towards the others.

"Well now, folks," Damien Blake addressed them, "Preston will probably fill you in on the details, but I'll just say this. In a few minutes, we're gonna do a trade with the Cheyennes. We've got a wagon stacked with rifles, and those renegades have enough gold to make the three of us rich. It's as simple as that!"

The emigrants stared open-eyed at the trio of gun-runners holding six-shooters on them.

"You—you filthy buzzards!" Janie Craig whimpered, drawing her children to her.

"I reckon that was exactly what Cutting said after he found out what those crates in our wagon were holding," Damien Blake mocked her.

"And you knifed him!" Abel Sorenson supplied.

"That's right, Preacher," Eli McKay complimented him sarcastically. "But don't worry—we ain't gonna do the same to you!"

Jonah's eyes blazed his fury. "What's it to be, then? Bullets for the lot of us, men, women and kids?"

"I'm not exactly sure, old goat," McKay said insultingly. "That'll be up to the Cheyennes."

Janie clutched her little girl closer to her body. "What do you mean?"

"Well, it's like this, ma'am," Damien Blake smiled. "In just a few minutes we'll be pulling our gun-wagon out to do the trade with our Indian friends, and I understand that this wagon train is first on their list for raiding. You see, no one's gonna be alive to tell the tale once those Cheyennes lay hands on those rifles! Hang on, there's a slight correction to that statement. Three prospectors will be riding west with a real sad story to tell. We'll be the sole survivors of a wagon train massacre."

"With saddlebags bulging with gold?" Shane remarked savagely.

"So once we got close to Gun Creek we did a little panning!" Blake smirked. "What's wrong with prospectors followin' their trade?"

"We're wastin' time," Reb Morton growled.

"Listen—*please,*" Janie Craig implored desperately. "There are *children* on this wagon train!"

Blake ignored her. "Eli ... the horses."

McKay stamped away, and Damien Blake grinned at Juanita. The 'breed girl gave him an icy stare.

"Mind you, there's just one person here I might be willing to take along with us, that's if she'll cooperate. Know what I mean, Juanita?"

"I'll take my chances with the others!" she blazed hotly.

"Suit yourself," Blake shrugged.

The settlers watched as McKay backed their team into harness. When this chore was completed, the gun-runner paced out to the corral. Standing together, the emigrants heard the thunder of McKay's guns, followed by his wild whooping. Dust billowed into the night sky from the corral, and as McKay emptied another gun, the terrified horses plunged up the slope. The spooked animals surged to the head of the crest, raced along the rim in panic-stricken flight and disappeared.

"You're making sure we're sitting ducks for the Cheyennes, aren't you?" Shane cracked.

McKay came ambling back into the camp and climbed up on the box of the gun-wagon.

"So long, folks," Blake smirked. "Been real nice having your company on the trail."

Still holding guns on the settlers, Blake and Morton backed to their wagon. Within seconds they had clambered aboard, and as McKay cracked the whip, the bulky prairie schooner swayed away from the camp carrying its evil cargo.

Shane cautioned the settlers about moving as Blake's gun muzzle was still pointed their way, but in a few moments, the team had pulled the wagon to the crest.

"Oh, God!" Janie Craig whispered frantically. "We're all going to die!"

The others raised their voices in lament.

"If we stay here like rats in a trap, we might as well start digging our graves now." Shane Preston held up his hand to silence them. "But we ain't sticking around. In fact, by the time those Indians come whooping down here, they'll find an empty camp."

Craig gaped. "But they've run off our horses! We can't just *walk* across the prairie!"

"Sure they ran off our horses," Shane said. "But the lead horse was my cayuse, and he won't be taking that herd too far."

The gunfighter stalked back to where his gun had fallen. He stooped down and picked up the cold comfort of his black six-shooter, shoving it into his holster. He could still hear the distant creak of the gun-wagon as he ran back to the frightened huddle of people in the center of the camp.

"Jonah," he drew the oldster aside, "while I'm rounding-up Snowfire, you get these folks ready for a long ride. All they'll be carrying is food, water, guns and ammunition. In five minutes I want them all dressed and ready."

"Five minutes!" the old-timer gulped.

"The Cheyennes mightn't give us much longer," Shane snapped.

Shane Preston loped away, heading through the wagons to the slope. He reached the crest, halting as he saw the white smudge of Blake's wagon still rolling into the night. Obviously the rendezvous was clear away from the camp, and he cursed as he imagined the scene which would take place somewhere out there on the prairie. Those renegade Cheyennes had been relatively harmless, carrying lances and ancient guns. But once in possession of modern rifles, they could set the whole frontier alight. And from what Blake had said, this wagon train of settlers was to be the first conflagration.

The gunfighter stood stock-still, his eyes searching the darkness.

He whistled long and low, giving the signal he knew Snowfire responded to. For years, the noble animal had been his constant companion, and Shane was confident that the palomino wouldn't let him down now. He whistled again, walking farther into the waving grass. At first, only the wind answered him, but then, as Shane listened, he heard a distant whicker. The gunfighter waited tensely as the thudding of hoofs sounded from the darkness. Moments later, the white horse came trotting towards him, its magnificent mane streaming out in the wind. Behind Snowfire came another, darker shape, and Shane recognized Jonah's aged mare lumbering out of the night. Seeing his master, Snowfire quickened its pace, snorting as it swept through the grass to the crest.

Shane remained still as Snowfire came right up to him, waiting as Tessie blundered awkwardly up to the crest.

He glanced out at the prairie and saw the shapes of other horses. These weren't exactly thundering up to the crest, but they'd followed Snowfire back, and now they milled tentatively around in the grass.

The gunfighter looked swiftly down at the camp. Barking orders like a general, Jonah Jones was organizing the settlers at the double. Even the Craig kids were running around, filling canteens with water, and Abel Sorenson jumped like a green trooper as the old-timer rasped out a command.

"Brett!" Shane yelled out to Craig as he emerged from his wagon. "You and the preacher grab some ropes and halters. There's horses to round up!"

The fugitive outlaw grabbed Sorenson, and together the two men loped up the slope of the hollow. Shane led Snowfire and Tessie into the camp, saddling them ready for the long trek ahead. Right in the center of the wagon square was a growing heap of guns and food, and when she'd dumped a saddle on the pile, Janie came over to him.

"Our wagons," she said. "What's going to happen to them?"

"They'd slow us down, so they stay here," Shane Preston told her. "Besides, a line of wagons can be seen from a helluva long way, and we have to be as inconspicuous as possible."

"All our possessions are in the wagon," Janie protested.

"No, ma'am," Shane countered, "your most important possessions are your kids, and they'll have a better chance of staying alive if we do things my way."

"Yes, of course," Janie conceded.

"Shane …" It was Juanita, who'd come to join them. "Tell me the truth! What sort of chance do we really have?"

Shane looked at her levelly.

"If we can make the high country before the Cheyennes hit us, a good chance. We'll be riding over hard rock in those ranges and our trail won't be easy for them to follow. But we'll have to move fast."

Even as he said this, Preacher Sorenson appeared on the rim of the hollow, struggling with two horses. Shane left the women, running up the slope to assist him. One of the horses, a big sorrel, was obviously still spooked, and the animal plunged violently. Shane seized the bridle and led the horse back down the slope.

"Can you still see the gun-wagon?" the gunfighter asked him.

Sorenson shook his head. "Nope, but we sure heard some whooping out there."

"Those renegades probably opening up the gun-cases," Shane muttered.

Craig topped the rise leading two more wagon-horses.

"We haven't got time to catch any more," Shane stated flatly as he waited for Brett Craig. "The kids and Juanita will have to ride double."

Busy hands saddled up, tied canteens to saddle horns and filled pouches with food. The settlers worked feverishly, and suddenly they heard the sharp crackle of gunfire out on the prairie. Then guns were blazing haphazardly and Shane knew that the gun-hungry Cheyennes were trying out the cargo Blake had brought for them.

"Mount up," Shane snapped. He stooped down by the weapon pile and handed a gun to Gloria Whittaker. She stuffed the .45 in the belt of her long riding dress. "All of you! Once those damn Indians get the smell of gunpowder, they'll get kill-crazy."

The Craig kids were hauled aboard. Tim Whittaker was grabbed by his mother and dumped in front of her. Abel Sorenson moved forward in the saddle and Juanita vaulted up behind him. With guns slotted in holsters, belts and saddlebags, and with food tied in sacks, the fugitives kicked their horses into a run.

Shane led the way out of the wagon circle, setting his hard face for the dark outline of the ranges. He rode swiftly, topping the hollow and striking out across the grass. The emigrants did not look back, lashing their horses away from the camp. Riding ahead, it was Shane who first saw the spread-eagled shape.

"Jonah," he called the oldster to him, "make sure Gloria keeps riding."

"Huh?"

Then the oldster saw the reason, and with a nod, he seized the woman's reins and spurred Tessie to move faster as Shane veered away from the line.

Shane headed over to the dark tangle of limbs and flesh. The long knife was buried to the hilt in Huss Whittaker's back, and the gunfighter felt anger in the pit of his belly as he glimpsed the bloodied mess at the crown of the wagon master's head. The savages had taken the body here to secure their grisly trophy. There was no time to stay, so Shane wheeled Snowfire, and the horse loped back to the others.

Wordlessly, they rode for the high country. Soon the plateau was broken up by deep ravines and long, grassy slopes that climbed towards the towering rims. Still Shane urged them on, not stopping to rest as they plunged through a pass. The horses slowed to a walk as the grassy ridge angled higher. Here and there patches of pumice rock stood out and Shane told the emigrants to ride over the hard rock to make their trail more difficult to follow.

The wind lashed them as they mounted the slope, a cold, biting wind from the north. The riders bowed their heads and wrapped coats and blankets around the kids. Shane led them higher, searching for the mouth of the pass—the gateway to the high country.

Finally he reined in under the knife-edged walls of the rock passage, and Shane turned in the saddle as the others filed up behind him.

"Look!" Sorenson pointed a quivering finger down at the prairie. "Fire!"

"They've put torches to the wagons," Shane murmured as the bitter wind whistled down the high pass.

There was a crimson glow in the darkness, and a vast pall of smoke was curling into the starlit sky. Tongues of fire were leaping wildly upwards, throwing out dancing shadows in the night. Shane glanced at the faces of the emigrants, sensing their frustration and feelings of defeat. They'd transported their treasured belongings all this way, through flood and desert, only to see them become a pyre so close to the Promised Land.

"Some of my books were priceless," Abel Sorenson whispered to Juanita as she clung to him on the horse. "But I did manage to bring one with me."

He patted his saddlebag.

"Your big Bible?" she guessed softly.

He shook his head.

"Jonah said it'd be too heavy and take up too much room," Sorenson said. "I've just a small New Testament in my saddlebag, one I received when I graduated."

"That's all you'll need when you start your new church in Gun Creek," Juanita said reassuringly, her hands clasped around his chest.

"*If* we reach Gun Creek," Abel Sorenson said.

"Abel," she spoke gently now, almost chidingly, "where's that faith of yours, the faith you preach about?"

He turned his head around, and momentarily their eyes met.

"Let's move," Shane said.

The walls of the pass rose sheer on both sides as the cavalcade pushed upwards. Here the clay had given way to solid rock, and the hoofs clattered as they rode. Once, the walls seemed almost to meet but there was a gap just wide enough for a horse, and one by one, they squeezed through. The floor of the pass became slippery, fed by tiny cascades of water trickling out of the rock face.

Quite suddenly, the pass widened dramatically.

Shane prodded Snowfire to the rim, sitting saddle as the pink fingers of sunrise began to stretch out over the high country. The darkness fled, and Shane lifted his eyes to the far-off peaks. The snow-coned mountains rose like a stockade, a dark, forbidding barrier, the last refuge of the bear and timber wolf. Shane picked out the narrow semblance of a trail along which he had intended taking the wagon train, but because the Cheyennes would probably consider that this would be the trail they'd follow, the scout decided to lead his charges straight across country, ignoring the known trail.

The fugitives headed into the new day, twisting down from the rim. They rode over a craggy stretch of rock, following Shane as he moved into a deep ravine. The sun showed above the eastern ridges as the wilderness beckoned the emigrants deeper into its rugged jaws.

The long day went by.

The noon heat was abating, and the shadows lengthening over the boulder-strewn canyon as the riders picked their way through. A great eagle swooped across their path, and from the cave-lined wall of the canyon, a mountain lion watched the travelers pass.

The horses were tired now, flecked with foam. A couple of them carrying two burdens began to stumble, and reluctantly, Shane raised his hand for a halt.

The emigrants dismounted wearily. Janie Craig slumped down on a boulder and wiped the grimy sweat from her face. Eager fingers unscrewed canteen tops, and Shane Preston stood apart from the others to build a cigarette.

"Jonah!"

The oldster ambled over, swigging what everyone else thought was water from his canteen. In actual fact, as Shane only knew, it was a mite more fiery than water and considerably stronger.

"What's on, pard?"

"Trouble catching up with us," Shane Preston told the oldster, keeping his voice low.

"Cheyennes?" The old gunslinger sounded almost casual.

"Seen them twice since noon," Shane murmured, poking the cigarette between his lips.

"Hell!" Jonah Jones grunted.

"Only saw a couple of them, but there could be others," the tall gunfighter informed him. "Last time I caught sight of them was when we moved into this canyon. The riders were behind us on that saw-tooth ridge, just sitting their ponies and watching."

"You never said anything," Jonah accused.

"I kept it to myself because I didn't want folks to panic," Shane muttered. "Anyway, the riders were too far away to start shooting at us. Listen, Jonah—there are women and kids here, not to mention a preacher man who's never fired a gun. I'm not gonna let them know about trouble until it's almost on us—that way there'll be no time for panic, only action."

"So what happens now?" Jonah took another swig from his canteen and some of the red liquid spilled down over his beard.

"I want to find out how many of them we have to face when the time comes," Shane said. He lit his cigarette.

"And that means I go take a look-see," the old-timer guessed with a grin.

"That's right, Jonah." Shane dragged on his cigarette and let his eyes wander over the Craig kids as they played around a clump of boulders. "When folks ask questions about you riding out, I'll just say you're checking. Okay?"

"When do I leave?"

"I reckon now's as good a time as any," Shane said quietly. "I'll be taking them west of that peak and we'll wait for you there, right under that black rock rim—"

Jonah's aged eyes picked out the landmark and he nodded.

"Don't get into any trouble," Shane advised him. "Unless—"

"Unless what?" Jonah asked suspiciously.

"If there's only a couple of 'em and you can pick 'em off with a rifle before they can make cover. Don't go tangling with the whole Cheyenne Nation!"

Jonah ran his hand through his mop of white hair.

"I aim to keep my scalp, so there's no chance of me playin' hero," Jonah said bluntly.

"See you in a couple of hours," Shane farewelled him.

He watched his trail-partner amble away to old Tessie and mount up. Jonah didn't look back as he headed down the canyon, and Shane waited as the emigrants clustered around him for an explanation.

"Figured it might pay for someone to check the back-trail." Shane sounded casual.

The folks glanced at each other.

"Check for—for Indian-sign, Shane?" Janie Craig spoke for them all.

Shane flicked the ash from his cigarette.

"Time to move on out," the gunfighter said.

"Damn grizzly!" Jonah Jones cursed as the mountain bear grunted and lumbered out of its cave.

The bear, disturbed in its lair by this bearded human, padded away in disgust and irritation. The huge animal clambered down the ledge and plunged into the brush below, while Jonah backed a little farther into the cave. The bear-stench was formidable, but Jonah pegged his nostrils with two fingers while he gradually accustomed himself to the odor.

He squatted down, using his elevated position to watch the entrance to the canyon. By now, the shadows were deepening, and the sun was merely a vague out-line in the west. Already the wind was chilled and the old gunfighter told himself that it would be a freezing night in the high country. He smoked a cigarette as he maintained his lofty vigil over the canyon.

Nothing moved below him.

Two cigarettes later, he edged a little closer to the entrance of the cave to survey the terrain beyond the canyon. It was wreathed in stillness. Yet not once did he question Shane's orders. He'd ridden with the black-garbed gun hawk for a long time, and if Shane said he'd seen Indians, they were out there some place, for sure.

Suddenly, he heard the dull thud of hoofs, and flat-tened himself against the wall of the cave. The sound seemed to come from right above the cave, and Jonah gripped his gun in a clenched fist as the hoof thuds reverberated through the hollow cavern. There was a long moment of silence, then a shadow fell over the mouth of the cave, and Jonah saw the Indian ride past. Just a few seconds later, more unshod hoofs came into view, and looking up, the old gun hawk gazed at the lean, copper-hued body of the rider. He glimpsed his hawk-like features as they slid past him. Sweat was breaking over Jonah's face as he realized that his plan to stake out high and watch the canyon below might have proved his undoing. The Indians had been keeping to the high ridges themselves, and now they were riding this ledge which hugged the valley wall.

Jonah crept to the entrance.

The riders would just be ahead of him on this narrow ledge, and two well-directed bullets would put an end to their menace once and for all. The hapless Cheyennes would have no room to maneuver and his slugs would cut them down.

Thus thinking, Jonah was about to sneak out onto a ledge when he was startled by the sound of more hoofs. Hastily, he drew back, melting into the shadows as first one, then three more bucks rode past the mouth of the cave.

He waited for fully two minutes before crawling cautiously to the ledge.

The Cheyenne braves were filing away from him now, and he breathed a long sigh of relief. He slid his gun into his holster, telling himself that he certainly wasn't about to take on six Indians. They were obviously a scouting party from the main bunch, and Jonah figured that the main force of the renegades would be following the normal trail. The oldster watched the riders picking their way along the ledge. Each man carried a rifle. There was no doubt that these scouts had seen the fugitives, and rather than return to fetch the main bunch, they were intending to grab all the glory for themselves.

Jonah waited until the last rider was out of sight.

He moved out of the cave and clambered down into the canyon.

Moving with surprising agility, Jonah ran through the brush below the cave, loping to the tree where he'd tethered Tessie. He swung into the saddle and headed to the verge of the rim. Somehow he had to sneak past those Cheyennes and get back to the emigrants.

SEVEN

HELL TRAIL!

Dusk was a gray shroud over the high country, dropping like a mist over the ridges. Already it held the towering rim in a darkening hand as Jonah slipped from his mount where Shane was waiting for him.

"Six of them," the old gun hawk announced. "Scouts from the main bunch, I reckon."

Shane glanced over to where the emigrants were eating together. There was no fire, but uncooked food was better than nothing at all. They were weary, and one of Janie's lads was fast asleep out of sheer exhaustion.

"Sure the main bunch is nowhere around?"

"Sure as I can be," Jonah said.

"Then we have to take care of these six scouts," Shane mused.

"All toting rifles, too," the oldster growled. "Shane—they ain't far away. Last time I saw them, they were moving this way under the peak."

Shane gazed up at the mountain. There was a long, low ridge which seemed to protrude right out of the side of the escarpment, and any riders heading for the rim would have to cross its flat face. In any case, the Indians would see their trail among the patches of pine needles they'd been unable to avoid.

"They're devils!" Jonah mouthed. "I watched them, Shane—saw them picking up our trail over hard rock!"

"They're Injuns, remember. Go grab yourself something to eat," said Shane.

The tall scout paced back to the emigrants who looked up at him expectantly.

"I want you all to listen carefully," he told them. "And then you'll do exactly what I say."

He looked at their tense faces and heard Abel Sorenson clear his throat nervously in the stillness.

"What is it, Shane?" Brett Craig asked.

"Jonah's just come back with a report," the gunslinger informed them. "There are six Cheyennes on their way here, right on our trail. Now, there's several things in our favor. One is they're just a scouting party, by all accounts, a long way from the main bunch. If we account for this lot, we probably won't even run into the rest. The other thing is they don't know that we're aware of them coming in."

"Oh, God!" Janie closed her eyes.

"Ma'am!" Shane's voice was suddenly harsh. "We've all got to keep calm!"

"I—I'm sorry!"

Brett Craig placed a protective arm around his wife's shoulders.

"We're going to stake out an ambush," Shane Preston told them. "You see that ridge? They'll be riding down it in just a short time, and that's where some of us will be waiting for them."

"Some?" Craig asked.

Shane ran his eyes over the emigrants.

"I want a fire built," the gunfighter commanded.

"A fire!" Preacher Abel Sorenson echoed. "But—but won't that attract them?"

"I'm hoping it will," Shane said. "In fact, Abel, you'll be right here under this rim with the women and kids, sitting round the fire—and you'll be in charge. I want it to look good and normal, just an ordinary camp. I'm hoping that the moment those varmints see the campfire, they'll have their eyes fixed on it so they won't see much else—until it's too late and we have them in our sights."

"In other words," Gloria Whittaker spelt out falteringly, "we're the bait in a trap."

"You could put it that way, Gloria," Shane admitted bluntly. "Our only chance is to set a trap for those renegades rather than let them creep up on us."

"Sounds sensible," Juanita agreed.

"But—but what if the ambush fails, and the Indians still ride in on the camp?" Janie shuddered.

Shane surveyed the women one by one with his cold eyes. For a while he said nothing.

"I want every one of you to have a loaded gun ready—just in case things don't go according to plan."

Juanita leapt to her feet, a long rifle in her hand. "And who'll be staked out on that ridge?" Juanita asked him fiercely.

"The menfolk," Shane returned. "All except Abel, and he'll be looking after things by the campfire."

"Shane!" the 'breed girl whispered. "You'll need more than three in that ambush!"

"Like I said, I decided that Abel should stay by the campfire," he grunted.

"I'm not talking about Abel." Juanita's breast heaved. "I can handle a rifle, Shane."

The gunfighter looked closely at her.

"All right," Shane conceded, after a pause, "you can come with us."

Sundown was a crimson streak as the pioneers hastily gathered wood for the fire. Abel Sorenson seemed like a man possessed, directing operations and personally lighting the dry pine cones under the larger pieces of timber.

Just before he walked away from the campfire, Shane called Gloria Whittaker aside.

"Gloria," he said, his tone low, "I'm saying this to you because I figure you're the best person to say it to, even though you've just suffered your loss."

"What is it, Shane?" the widow asked.

"If the worst happens," the gunfighter said, "you know what someone has to do."

Gloria looked past him at the darkness of the ridge, and then she nodded. She'd lived too long on the frontier and heard too many stories of rape and torture not to know the answer.

"I know what I must do," she stated gently. "No woman or child must be taken alive. Leave it to me, Shane."

He stalked away from her. Behind him, tongues of fire were leaping and crackling through the heap of timber. Juanita was waiting with the two men. Shane nodded to them, and they began to strike out for the ridge. They climbed the slope in silence, and finally Shane stood on the flat top. He motioned them into a crevice that crossed the rock face diagonally, and they slithered down the gritty sides.

Shane glanced back at the camp.

The fire down there would be seen all the way from the peak, and he had no doubt that the six Indians would already have spotted the fiery glow.

The wagoners didn't have long to wait.

It was Shane's sharp eyes which picked out the ghostly shadows in the gloom. They were filtering down the ridge, gray shapes of men molded to their ponies, and Shane's warning was a soft whisper in the last glow of sundown. Hands clutched guns. Brett Craig stroked the cold length of his rifle. Juanita stood there coolly, her eyes fixed on the oncoming Cheyennes. Old Jonah glanced aside at Shane. They'd been in tighter spots than this before, but never had the lives of so many women and kids depended on them.

They could hear the guttural voices of the riders. One of the renegades, a huge, near-naked Cheyenne, was pointing at the fierce glow of the campfire. They rode closer and, slowly, Shane Preston began to level his Winchester.

Shane squinted down the sights, drawing a bead on the massive renegade at their head. The ponies were jogging nearer to the crevice, and the gunfighter could distinguish the copper faces and black hair of the oncoming scouts. The Indians halted their ponies, drawing together to discuss and nod towards the campfire.

"Take them!" Shane's command was a whip-crack in the dusk.

Four guns boomed in deadly unison from the crevice and a wall of screaming lead splattered into the milling renegades. The giant rider crumpled as a bullet smashed into his chest, and the pinto pony reared when the Indian plunged downwards and sprawled on the rock. Another Cheyenne had been shot in the face, and his hands were two bloodied claws digging into his ruptured flesh. Shane's second slug lifted the dying man clean off his pony, and he joined the beefy Indian on the ridge. In desperation, the other renegades wheeled their ponies. They grappled with their newly-acquired rifles, and one lean Indian fired his as he veered sideways. The bullet ripped into the top of Brett Craig's shoulder, and the fugitive dropped against the wall of the dip. Craig's gun slithered down as the outlaw's right hand tried to stem the gushing blood-flow.

Juanita's gun belched a second time, and the renegade who'd just blasted Craig caught her bullet in his hip. The Indian's eyes bulged with pain, and suddenly he urged his pony right at the crevice on a suicidal charge. Jonah raised his rifle and fired, and the bullet lifted him clean off his pony.

The last three renegades were pumping bullets at them now, riding to one side as they kept low and blasted haphazardly at the crevice. Shane heard the

124

'breed girl gasp in agony right alongside him, and glancing towards her, the gunfighter glimpsed the dark stain across the front of her blouse. She slumped down, groaning and holding on to his body. Shane leveled his gun over her head at the Cheyenne who'd plugged her, and the brave's throaty cry rang out as the bullet tore into his chest. The last two renegades shouted hoarsely to each other, gesticulating in near panic.

Jonah threw away his empty Winchester and lifted his six-shooter from its holster. Both of the gun slicks fired simultaneously and one of the renegades crashed to the ground with a burning slug in his back. The last rider fled into the night with the gunfighters blasting the void until their gun-hammers fell on empty chambers.

"Damn it to hell!" Shane stood up, jamming a cartridge into his loading chamber. "Look after things here while I go after that last one, Jonah."

The tall gunfighter climbed out of the crevice and whistled for his horse. Snowfire was just down from the ridge, and the palomino trotted up the slope as Shane ran to meet him and vaulted onto the stallion's back. Gloria and Janie were hurrying towards the ridge to assist with the wounded as Shane urged Snowfire into the night. No questions were directed at him, because every emigrant realized the emergency that had arisen. If that renegade made it back to the main bunch, the war-party would soon be here to butcher them all. That last scout had to die.

Shane rode Snowfire past the bloodied bodies of the Indians, heading farther up the flat-top ridge. The Cheyenne had vanished, but Shane figured that the scout would retrace his trail in order to ride straight back to the main bunch. The stallion responded to Shane's touch, and heeling it fiercely, the gunfighter mounted the ridge. By now, the dying sun had surrendered to nightfall, and a wan moon was rising in the blackness. Soon, pallid light was drenching the ridge, and the rocks cast strange shadows as Shane rode higher.

Suddenly he heard the sharp rasp of metal on rock.

Instinctively, Shane Preston threw himself from his horse's back, and his body crashed onto the hard rock a split-second before the rifle screamed. The bullet winged high over Snowfire, and as Shane rolled for the cover of a boulder, he saw the glimmer of steel in the moonlight. The renegade had heard his approach and was staked out ready for him behind a pyramid of boulders.

Shane scrambled behind the rock. He thumbed back the hammer of his gun and waited. Gradually, he eased his gun around the rock but moments later the rifleman fired at him and the lead tore splinters of pumice from the boulder.

"Can you hear me?" Shane's yell sounded above the fading echoes of the gunshot.

There was no answer, but Shane figured that the renegade understood him. These Cheyennes had been on a Reservation, and they would know the white man's language.

"Hear me, redman!" Shane called to him.

His answer was a whining slug that sang off into the night sky.

"I've got all the time in the world!" Shane told him. "But you haven't, redman! You're a long way from your other braves, but my friends are just down that ridge! Already they'll have heard the shooting, and more will be here soon! Better climb down and kill me so you can ride on your way—while you can."

There was a deep hush, and Shane edged his face around the rock. The Cheyenne mightn't have understood every word, but he'd grasped enough of the logic to realize he had to act now. In fact, the renegade's tanned body was sliding down the rocks. Shane wormed around so he lay flat on his belly.

The Cheyenne crouched at the foot of the pile of boulders. His beady eyes surveyed the lonely rock behind which the gunfighter was waiting for him.

Shane raised his gun.

The Indian began to circle, hoping to sneak up on Shane from the side, but the gunfighter's cold eyes followed him—and so did his gun muzzle.

Then the renegade halted. He hesitated before gliding towards the side of the rock. Shane meanwhile had slithered around to face him, and he leveled his six-shooter at the oncoming shadow. The Cheyenne seemed to loom up out of the ridge. Two pairs of eyes met. Two guns thundered. The Indian's bullet carved a furrow in the rock beside Shane's head, but the gunfighter's slug sliced like a knife into the red man's heart.

Shane climbed to his feet and looked down at the body.

He walked over to where Snowfire was waiting for him, mounted up and rode back to the camp.

"I've cut Brett's slug out." The fire glow reddened Jonah's whiskery face as he glanced up at the towering gunfighter. "It wasn't in that deep, though it smashed some of his shoulder bone. I've taken out some of the splinters, but I'll leave the rest for the medic at Fort Defiance."

"And Juanita?" Shane asked him.

"Janie's plugged her wound," the oldster gulped.

"But her bullet?" Shane demanded.

Jonah Jones swallowed and he stood up to face his partner.

"It's in too deep," Jonah said, his tone blunt. "I couldn't risk cutting it out."

Shane stalked around the other side of the campfire. The women had made the girl as comfortable as possible, propping her up on a makeshift pillow of saddlebags, and covering her with two blankets. She was still conscious, and Shane saw the dark trickle of blood ooze from the corner of her mouth as she tried to speak.

"Easy, Juanita," he said softly, crouching down beside her.

Somehow, Shane's presence seemed to reassure her, and the wounded girl forced a faint smile.

She watched him intently as his hand gently pulled away the bloodied shreds of her blouse, exposing the swell of her left breast and the ugly crater just above.

"Janie," Shane murmured, "water and clean linen."

They'd already heated some water over the fire, and Janie Craig simply lifted her riding dress and tore a length off her petticoat. Shane grabbed the linen, dabbed it in the water, and began to wash away the blood from her flesh. Her firm breasts heaved as the pain raced through her like a tide. Shane bent over her, his eyes taking in the dark outline of the bullet deep beneath the surface of her flesh.

"Juanita," the gunfighter said, "the slug's in one helluva long way. Now, you can wait till we reach Fort Defiance or—"

"Or what, Shane?" Her whisper was barely audible.

"Or you can take a chance and I'll cut it out now," the gunfighter said.

Her trembling hand reached out of the blankets and gripped his. He looked hard at her and saw the trust in her eyes, the kind of trust most women reserve for only one man in life.

"Cut it out," Juanita Woolrich summoned the strength to say.

Shane stood up.

"Jonah!"

The old-timer climbed to his feet and left Craig. He bustled around the campfire.

"I want you to give Juanita some of that special fire-water you carry in your canteen," Shane said dryly. "Reckon it'll help deaden the pain."

Jonah flushed as the emigrants thrust him quizzical looks. He ambled to his saddle and unhooked his canteen. Meanwhile, Shane drew his knife out and placed the blade deep into the fire to cauterize it. He waited while Jonah knelt down beside the girl and gently tipped the canteen to her lips.

"Shane," Abel Sorenson murmured as the gunslick watched the blade glow red.

"What is it?"

"I—I feel so helpless," the preacher admitted. "What can I do to help?"

The red was turning to white.

"I'm not a praying man, Abel." Shane kept his eyes on the knife. "But you are."

Shane took hold of the wooden handle of his blade and crouched down beside the whisky-drugged girl.

Her eyes were blurred and the bewildered emigrants frowned as Jonah bemoaned his empty canteen.

"Hold her," Shane commanded.

Someone slid a piece of wood between Juanita's teeth just before Shane's knife delved into the wound. Juanita stiffened, squirming and moaning, but relentlessly, Shane moved the knife in farther. The sharp point probed deeper, and with a shudder, Juanita passed out. The gunfighter found the lethal slug, and without taking out the knife, he continued to dig. Finally the point reached the base of the bullet and Shane began to prise the lead upwards. The emigrants watched in silence as their trail scout eased the bullet to the surface. The thumb and forefinger of Shane's left hand gripped the slug and pulled it free. Blood gushed out over her flesh and Shane held out his hand for linen. Another piece of Janie's petticoat was handed to him, and it was used to plug the wound. Shane lowered his head to the girl's bosom. Her heart was still thudding, and he could hear a tiny moan escape her lips.

"Bandage her tight and keep her warm," he directed the women. "She has a chance to live."

EIGHT

FORT DEFIANCE

"Major Bentley will see you now," the stiff-lipped adjutant said as Shane dusted his Stetson against his thigh.

The soldier opened the door for him, and Shane Preston stepped inside the log-walled office. The moment he entered, a lean, lynx-eyed man stood up from his desk chair and extended a gaunt hand.

Shane shook it warmly.

"Nice to see you again, Preston," Major Bentley said. "Take a seat."

"I'll stand, thanks," Shane said, meaning to make this interview as brief as possible.

"Suit yourself," the soldier shrugged.

Bentley slumped back in his chair and reached for his pipe. He'd been commander of this outpost for several years, and this was the third time he'd met up with the gunfighter who'd blazed a legendary trail across his territory. Last time, Bentley had tried to persuade Shane Preston to don a uniform, but the tall rider had politely declined.

"Didn't expect to see you riding in with those emigrants," Major Bentley confessed. "In fact, I was just about to roster a burial detail to ride out there and find the bodies."

"Then three men rode in with the news?" Shane asked him.

Bentley stuffed tobacco into his pipe. "Three prospectors, Preston. They said they were here to report a wagon massacre and they said they were the sole survivors."

"And those three men rode on to Gun Creek?" Shane recalled Blake's boast.

"Yes." Bentley frowned. "I remember what one of them said. They had to take another trail here to escape the renegade Cheyennes after everyone else on the wagon train had been butchered—but by taking that trail, they struck it lucky. They camped in a dry wash and found some nuggets. In fact, they left the fort yesterday to cash their gold in Gun Creek, and I reckon right now they'll be celebrating there."

"They received the gold from the Cheyennes," Shane said tersely. "In exchange for the latest repeating rifles. On top of that, they left the wagoners to get killed by those gun-crazy renegades."

"My God!" Bentley stared at him then jumped to his feet and listened in silence as Shane recalled what had happened. Grim-faced, Bentley heard the whole story, and when Shane had finished, he walked over to the big map nailed to his wall.

"And where do you figure these Reservation-jumpers are?" he asked.

"Send out a whole platoon, Major," Shane advised him, standing by the map and indicating where he believed Vittorio's bunch would be. "Those red devils aren't gonna be too easy to round up now they're toting those guns."

"Thanks to those three bastards!" Bentley rasped. "Hell! I'll get some men to ride into Gun Creek now and fetch them here."

"Oh no!" Shane raised his hand.

"Huh?"

"Those varmints are ours, Major," Shane said grimly. "You and your soldier-boys can fix the Cheyennes, but me and Jonah have a score to settle with those gun-runners."

Bentley stared at him.

"They murdered a real good friend of mine, Major," Shane explained. "Wagon master Huss Whittaker."

"And so you'll be taking the law into your own hands?" the soldier demanded.

"Yes, Major," Shane Preston stated bluntly. "And don't try to stop us."

134

Bentley picked up his pipe and his keen eyes surveyed Shane as he struck a match. He crossed over to the window and gazed out over the dusty parade-ground. The emigrants were seated on the porch outside the store, and two soldiers were supplying them with food and coffee. The kids, now safe, played around the tall flagpole in the center of the yard. Ten minutes ago, they'd summoned the fort doctor who was examining Brett Craig and the 'breed girl inside the small hospital.

"You know, Preston," Bentley said, puffing on his pipe, "gun-running's a military offence, so I'll want to know exactly how you—uh—deal with the culprits. Just for the report, you understand."

"Sure," Shane grinned. "We'll drop by after we've dealt with them—just for your report's sake."

"There are three of them, you know," Bentley warned him as he made for the door.

"They don't know we're coming," Shane growled.

He paced outside and jammed his Stetson onto his head. The adjutant saluted him, but Shane took no notice as he walked across the sunlit parade ground.

Jonah was waiting for him.

"Those renegades will soon be back in the Reservation," Shane predicted confidently. "Meantime, we've got one small chore to take care of."

The two gun hawks strode across to their horses.

They mounted up and headed towards the double entrance gates. Four troopers pulled the heavy gates wide, and the gunfighters urged their horses out of the stockade onto the dusty plain.

The mid-afternoon sun blazed in their faces as they turned west along the rutted trail. Shane and Jonah rode away from the military outpost, following the ribbon of trail as it wound around an ancient butte and dropped from sight over a black rock ridge. Once at the crest of this ridge, they reined in their horses and sat saddle, surveying the settlement sprawled below.

"The Promised Land." Jonah used the emigrants' phrase.

"And built nice and close to Fort Defiance in case of any emergency," Shane Preston remarked dryly. "Let's get down there."

"Say, Shane," the old gunslinger grinned. "I reckon we've got company."

Shane turned in the saddle. There was a rider heading their way from the shadows of the fort, a spiral of swirling dust in his wake. The two gun hawks waited as Abel Sorenson spurred his horse towards them and reined in alongside.

"Heard you were riding to Gun Creek," the preacher said. "Figured you wouldn't mind if I came along."

"Listen, Abel," Shane snapped, "this ain't exactly a camp-meetin' we're riding to."

"I know why you're headed for Gun Creek," Abel Sorenson said quietly. "But that's not my reason for joining you."

"Oh?" Shane muttered.

"I figured I'd come along to look over the town," the preacher informed them.

Shane's wizened sidekick scowled. "This ain't a sight-seein' expedition."

"I'm not riding in to sight-see, gentlemen," Sorenson smiled. "I'll be looking around for vacant plots, suitable for the site of my future church."

"Aren't you looking a mite too far ahead?" Shane asked the pioneer preacher.

"Shane," Sorenson sat tall and straight in the saddle, like he was giving out a pulpit announcement. "By next fall, my chapel will be Gun Creek's house of worship."

Shane grinned and flicked his reins. The stallion ambled down the slope, and with Jonah and the preacher right behind him, Shane set his face for Gun Creek.

The trail was steep, fringed with craggy rocks, and it spilled out of the boulders into a long, wide valley. The new settlement of Gun Creek loomed up and soon the riders were passing a line of shacks. A huge hand-painted signboard announced GUN CREEK, and farther on, another board told all and sundry that the cheapest liquor and the best saloon-girls could be found at the Golden Garter.

The riders moved into the wide street, heading past two sets of hastily-erected buildings. Some of the pioneers had simply planted their wagons along the edges of the street, and more than one home had been built onto the side of a prairie schooner. There were more substantial buildings, like the Cattlemen's Bank and the Town Hall, and the Golden Garter was a big two-storey complex of iron and clapboard. The saloon front was painted a gaudy gold, but the paintwork had been marred by mud-splashes. There was, as Shane had been informed, no law in Gun Creek. The residents had built a jailhouse, and work had commenced on a law office, but a large notice swung from the tie rail out front.

WANTED—THE FIRST SHERIFF OF GUN CREEK.
$60 per month.
APPLY TO MAYOR FREDERICK CANDICE

It was a primitive community. No boardwalks lined the street, and the gun hawks rode their horses in deep dust which would become a quagmire after rain. An old tub served as a water trough. There were two general stores, and the smallest one had no window—just a big aperture in the front wall. Shane noticed that the alleys branching away from Front Street were mostly lined by lean-to shacks and the remains of wagons.

Gun Creek in its present condition reminded Shane of the northern boom towns which sprang up around a gold strike, but he told himself that as more emigrants poured west and settled around the town, amenities would follow. Sorenson was probably right. Next fall there would be a church. He glanced aside at the preacher. Abel Sorenson had lost some of his starchiness on the long trek, and Shane now admired the man. The preacher, too, was a pioneer, and it would take a measure of courage to build a church in a raw, rough town like Gun Creek.

Shane reined in beside a gaily-painted wagon which almost straddled the street. A portly little man wearing a bow-tie, silk shirt, and matching gray pants and derby, beamed at the three strangers. Arrayed on a long shelf attached to the length of his wagon was a variety of bottles and cans.

"Good afternoon, gents," the travelling salesman boomed. "Can I interest you in salts for the liver, tonic water, liniment or maybe pills guaranteed to prevent fever before it strikes you? The name, by the way, is Adam Buckle, travelling doctor, and since there is no medico in Gun Creek and folks have to travel to Fort

Defiance for treatment, then you would do well to stock up on medicinals."

Shane picked up one of his bottles of red tonic water and noted the price was one dollar.

"Of course," Adam Buckle murmured confidentially, "should you prefer some—er—good strong brandy, for medicinal purposes only, you understand, then right here in my wagon I have the very best you can buy—"

"Mr. Buckle," Shane addressed the salesman, "maybe I'll come back and take a look-see at your wares, but first I'd like a little information."

"Ask away." Adam Buckle puffed out his chest.

"We're looking for three men—prospectors," Shane told him.

"Blake, Morton and McKay," Adam Buckle recited.

The gunslingers exchanged glances at the swift reply, and Abel Sorenson frowned.

"You seem to know who we're looking for," Shane murmured.

"Everyone's looking for Blake, Morton and McKay," the salesman grinned. "So I naturally assumed that you were, too. Most everyone I talk to is looking for those three gentlemen."

"Why's that?" Jonah demanded.

"They struck it rich!" The salesman spread his hands. "They cashed their gold nuggets and it's been drinks on the house in the Golden Garter ever since last night. Mind you, I figure they can afford it! The bank manager happened to let slip that those three lucky prospectors banked enough money from the sale of those nuggets to set them up for life! They're mighty popular boys right now—in fact, since they're buying drinks all round, you could say they're this town's heroes!"

"Heroes!" Sorenson said indignantly.

"Pity about that wagon train they were travelling on, however. But then, it goes to show how in spite of tragedy, Lady Luck can shine on honest men."

The preacher was about to blurt out something, but Jonah cautioned him with a soft word.

"You're—ah—friends of the three prospectors?" Adam Buckle asked.

"We know them," Shane said.

"Well," Buckle nodded over at the saloon, "you'll find them in the Golden Garter—been there since last night, celebrating. First time the saloon's been open all night in the history of Gun Creek!"

"A painted Jezebel!" Sorenson exclaimed as a scantily-clad saloon girl sauntered out of the Golden Garter.

She was a vivacious redhead dressed in a low-cut flimsy gown and she stood in front of the swinging batwings with a challenging air. Jonah grinned at her but Sorenson snorted in disgust.

"Jezebel!" Sorenson repeated.

"You a Bible-thumper, or something, mister?" Adam

Buckle frowned at him.

"The Lord has guided me here to build a church," Abel Sorenson stated. "And to speak out against dens of iniquity!"

Buckle reached for one of his medicinal brandies and took a swift swig.

"I wish you luck, Reverend," the salesman gulped. "Because you're gonna damn well need it!"

The three riders left the travelling salesman to mutter to himself and crossed the street to where at least thirty horses and rigs were lining the tie rails.

"Abel," Shane murmured, "I reckon it's about time for you to go looking for vacant plots."

Sorenson glanced at Shane and Jonah. There was a coldness in their eyes, and he saw that their hands were resting on their gun butts. They were men who were about to ply their trade, and in a very short while there would be death in Gun Creek.

"Maybe—maybe this isn't exactly good theology," Sorenson whispered, "but I'll be praying for you."

"You do that," Shane murmured.

They could hear the clink of glasses and loud, raucous laughter coming from inside the Golden Garter, and the redhead outside the batwings gave them a welcome smile. Shane ignored her as he slipped from Snowfire's back.

"Howdy, boys!" the percentage girl greeted them. "Strangers in town?"

"Yeah," said Shane. Someone had started to play the piano in the saloon, and the jigging notes were wafted out over the batwings.

"Then welcome to the Golden Garter," said the girl, her frank eyes moving over Shane Preston in an appreciative manner. "You've come at the right time, boys! Drinks are free—paid for by the most popular three fellers ever to set foot in Gun Creek! In fact, if you're hankering to spend some time with a lady like me, then those generous prospectors might even pay for that if you just ask them. They're loaded with cash, boys! But you'll have to hurry. You see, they're planning to leave town soon, could be sundown."

Shane eased past her and stood at the batwings.

The Golden Garter was full to capacity. There was a heaving sea of men inside, drinking, gambling, laughing and dancing with percentage girls. Liquor was flowing like a river from two wooden barrels perched on the bar counter, and saloon patrons were lining up to recharge their glasses. A bald-headed man was clowning at the piano. Shane ran his gaze over the patrons. Most of them were bearded, hard-bitten pioneers relishing the free liquor and singing the praises of their benefactors. For the three killers, however, this was merely a token gesture, and the cost to them would be small compared with the loot they had just lodged in the bank. Not understanding the real value of white man's gold, the renegades had paid dearly for their rifles.

Shane's eyes found McKay. He was swigging a bottle of redeye at the center table, and perched on his lap was an underage saloon girl. Right behind him, guffawing and joking with several men, stood Reb Morton. Shane searched for Damien Blake, finally finding him over at the bar, surrounded by drinking patrons. The gun-runners were enjoying themselves, whooping it up with the proceeds of the gold.

"What's your name?" Shane asked the girl.

"Anita," she pouted.

"And where's your room, Anita?"

"Upstairs," Anita smiled seductively. "Number Five. Right on the balcony. Why, mister? You planning on spending some time with me?"

Shane took out a wad of bills from his pocket and Anita's eyes glowed like stars.

"What's more," he said, "I don't have to ask those three prospectors to pay you. I'm a man who pays for his own female company."

"Follow me," she smiled.

Anita made sure she brushed tantalizingly against him as she swayed for the batwings.

"There's just one thing," Shane arrested her.

"Oh?"

"I'm a mite shy," the gunfighter said in a whisper.

She placed a soft hand on his arm. "Don't worry, mister! I'm an expert at handling shy men!"

"I mean," he said hastily, "I'm too shy to walk with you right through that saloon and up the stairs with everyone looking on and—well—knowing what I'm going for!"

She frowned, then brightened.

"Look, mister," she said, her hand still toying with his arm, "this is strictly against the rules, you understand, but with a special case like you, I'm willing to make an exception. I'll take you in the rear entrance and up the back stairs that lead to my room."

"I sure am grateful, Anita," Shane grinned warmly. Anita planted her hands on her hips and scrutinized him with a long stare.

"You know, you don't *look* the shy type!"

"But I am," he reassured her.

"Come on, then."

"I'll just have a word with my sidekick first," Shane excused himself.

He turned towards the grinning Jonah.

"Just mosey inside and keep your head down," the tall gunfighter told him. "Don't attract the attention of those three killers."

"And you?"

"You'll see me on the balcony when I'm ready," the tall gunfighter said aside.

"Well," the oldster chuckled softly, "don't get lost in that filly's room!"

Shane turned and followed the percentage girl along the front of the saloon, moving with her down the side alley.

Sorenson, who hadn't as yet left, was looking aghast. "Don't worry, Abel," Jonah grinned. "Shane's safe. He doesn't hanker after redheads!"

Leaving the preacher standing by his horse, Jonah Jones slipped unobtrusively between the batwings. He spotted a vacant table in the far corner, and slouched to it through the sawdust and empty liquor bottles.

Jonah slumped down on a chair, head lowered. He placed his gun on his lap under the table.

NINE

TRAIL'S END SHOWDOWN

"Well, now," Anita purred as she closed the side door, "how about a drink first?"

"Rye," Shane said, as she crossed the pink carpet to the liquor closet beside her bed.

This was no ordinary whore's room, he told himself. It was spotlessly clean, and his eye was taken by the satin bedspread that stretched alluringly on her four-poster. There was a hand-carved dressing table, and in front of this, a mahogany stool and two chairs.

But Shane only gave the furnishings a brief glance as his attention became fixed on the other door right opposite the street window. Anita had obligingly led him up the side passage and they'd entered by the door next to the dressing table, but now he looked long and hard at the other one.

"That door," she murmured, seeing his attention focused on the latch, "leads onto the balcony, and a shy man wouldn't want to walk out there."

She swayed towards him with a glass of whisky.

"Now, mister," she said, getting down to business straight away, "there's the small matter of paying me …"

He pulled out ten dollars and placed them on her dressing table. She lowered her eyes, sitting at the mirror and brushing her flaming hair while Shane downed his drink in a single gulp.

"Well, mister," she said, swiveling around on her stool, figuring it was time to drop the small-talk, "whenever you're ready."

But Shane had lifted the latch, and when she saw the black-handled six-shooter in his hand, Anita stifled a scream.

"Just stay right here, ma'am," the gunfighter ordered her.

He edged outside onto the balcony and closed the door.

The saloon uproar rose to meet him, and as he padded to the head of the stairs, he saw the source of the current merriment. An old-timer, obviously under the influence of too much whisky, was stomping on the bar counter. Now, the folks had probably seen such antics before, but this time a touch of spice had been added. The old fool had taken off his Levis, and was dancing in his long, woolen underwear. Suddenly he slipped and crashed into the crowd who helped him to his feet and heaved him back onto the bar.

Shane's eyes went to the big oil-lamp chandelier hanging above the saloon floor.

Still no one had noticed him as he leveled his six-shooter and thumbed back the hammer. He squeezed the trigger and the thunder rocked the Golden Garter. A saloon girl screamed hysterically as the chandelier plummeted down and crashed into the crowd. Drinkers and tinhorns scrambled away as glass flew in all directions. Light from the wall-lamps was enough to illuminate the scene. Then a deep hush settled over the Golden Garter, as every eye looked up at the tall man dressed in black and holding his six-shooter with smoke curling from the muzzle.

"Hell!" McKay's exclamation broke the silence as he stared upwards at the gunfighter.

Morton whimpered, staring white-faced as if he were looking at a ghost. "Preston!"

"Blake! Morton! McKay!" Shane spat out the names with cold vehemence. "Stand clear of the crowd!"

Damien Blake was shaking, but nevertheless, he was the first gun-runner to tread into the space cleared when the falling chandelier sent the patrons scurrying. Reb Morton followed him, eyes still bulging his disbelief, and last of all McKay came and stood tentatively beside his companions.

"What in the hell's goin' on?" a towner yelled from the gaping crowd.

Shane pointed his gun at Blake. "I'll tell you what's going on! I've come to deal with three murdering gunrunners who sold rifles to the Cheyennes!"

A murmur floated through the crowd.

"Men of Gun Creek!" Damien Blake kept his hand conspicuously away from his gun as he addressed them confidently. "I'll tell you who this man is and why he's acting loco! He's had a grudge against me and my boys for years, and at last he's caught up with us! Now, you can believe his fool story about gunrunning if you like—or you can help me get rid of him and we'll return to our fun! Remember, we're the boys who've been paying for your drinks!"

"And you're the boys who gave the Cheyennes rifles for their gold," Shane Preston grated.

"What the heck are you talkin' about, mister?" the towner yelled again. "These are three prospectors who survived a wagon train massacre and who happened to strike it rich on their way here."

"I've heard what their story is," Shane stated grimly. "Now I'll tell you the truth and you can all stand aside while I deal with them. These lousy polecats used a wagon train to run rifles to the Indian renegades, leaving the emigrants to die while they rode off with the Cheyenne gold."

"Blake!" McKay rapped. "Shut him up—"

"You can't prove that!" Damien Blake challenged.

"That's where you're wrong, Blake." The gun was steady in Shane's iron fist. "There are emigrants now at Fort Defiance who'll back up my story and confirm what stinking liars you three are. And it's quite easy for the citizens of this town to prove for themselves. *It's a real short ride to Fort Defiance.*"

"Gun-running's a serious offence," a stubble-faced towner spoke up. "Reckon we owe it to ourselves to check out his story."

"Meantime," another patron grunted, "we could lock these men up in the jail. It's as good a time as any to give that cell block its baptism."

"Listen—all of you!" Damien Blake spoke strongly. "We've been buying you drinks! We're your friends! What the heck has that no-account saddle bum ever done for you?"

The saloon patrons were edging away now, and suddenly the three prospectors stood very much alone in the center of the saloon with the shattered pieces of the chandelier sprinkled around them. Blake looked around desperately at the men he'd spent money on, but there was no sympathy on their faces.

"I'm riding to the fort," someone said at the batwings. "I'll check out the truth and come back in a few minutes."

Ashen-faced, the gun-runners exchanged frantic glances.

"Take the bastard!" Blake whispered.

McKay groped for his gun, and Morton glanced around wildly as he too slapped leather. There was a wild, hysterical scream from one of the saloon girls as Shane's six-shooter belched. The bullet smashed into Eli McKay's ribs, carrying him backwards over a poker table. The chips and cards flew, and as men fled farther away, McKay dropped like a log in the sawdust.

Morton's gun boomed from the hip, and the tall gunfighter darted to one side as the bullet ripped into the satin drapes behind him. Suddenly another shot thundered from the body of the saloon, and Reb Morton caught a bullet in the side of his head. Clawing the wound, he spun around, firing again as Jonah stood there with a smoking gun in his hand.

The second slug from the killer's gun bored into Jonah's shoulder, and the old-timer clutched it with a yelp. Like a wounded animal at bay, Jonah Jones backed as he fired twice in rapid succession. Two black craters opened in Morton's chest and he died on his feet, finally to crumple down and sprawl at Damien Blake's boots.

Blake hadn't moved.

The gun-runner had his hands high, and he smirked at Shane as he came slowly down the stairs.

"You won't shoot a man who's surrendered, Preston," Blake grinned mirthlessly.

"I'll holster my gun," Shane said in the deep hush, "then you make your play, Blake."

"Too bad, Preston. I'm crippled as of now!"

Blake deliberately let his right hand trail to the buckle of his gun rig.

He unfastened the rig, and it slithered round his hips and finally dropped.

"I'm a prisoner," Blake announced. "That is, Preston—unless you want to kill me in cold blood?"

Shane cocked his gun hammer. Blake was smiling, mocking him, knowing full well that the gunfighter's code would prevent him from pulling the trigger.

"There's a cell block over the street," Shane said. "Walk!"

"With pleasure!" the gun-runner laughed.

Shane's eyes narrowed to twin slits of hatred as he marched the killer to the batwings. Behind him, old Jonah was slumped in a chair trying to stem the flow of blood from his wounded shoulder. Shane reached the doors, and Damien Blake parted them ahead of him. The gunfighter prodded him onto the street into the dying sun, and with his hands high, Blake sauntered across the dust. Folks ran to open the door of the cell block and faces were pressed against the glass of the Golden Garter as they watched Shane shove the prisoner right into the center of the street.

"Hold it!" The snarl froze Shane Preston in his tracks. *"Hold it right there, Preston, or I'll blast you to hell!"*

A frog-like figure straddling his dust-streaked horse was to his left, and Shane glimpsed the long shadow of a Winchester pointed at him.

"It's been a long, hard trail, Preston!" Matt Woolrich grated. "But when my bullet's in your head, it'll sure be worth it!"

"Stay outa this, Woolrich," Shane warned him. "This ain't your fight. Let me lock this gun-runner in his cell, and then I'll come out and we'll talk things over."

"Oh no," Woolrich said bleakly. "You took my woman, and I swore I'd find you and her! Took a helluva long trail and a bit of luck when I asked some questions in Conchita, but here I am—and from all accounts, my woman is real close by."

"That's another matter!" Shane insisted.

"Maybe it isn't," Matt Woolrich said. He stared long and hard at the gunfighter's captive. "I don't know who you are, mister, but anyone being herded by Preston is a friend of mine. Now, step away from him—and Preston, if you so much as try anything, I'll blast you apart!"

Damien Blake moved briskly to one side.

"Mister," Blake addressed Woolrich, "I reckon you and me'll get on just fine, and I've got enough money to make us both rich."

"That sounds real interestin'," Woolrich drawled. "There's a gun for you in my saddlebag."

Damien Blake ambled towards the rider, and the towners stared nonplussed at this bewildering turn of events.

"Now for you, Preston." Matt Woolrich looked down the barrel of his rifle. "Let that gun drop."

Reluctantly, Shane opened his fingers, and the notched six-shooter slid into the dust.

Damien Blake was rummaging through the saddlebag, and elation sprang to his face as his fingers gripped the butt of a gun.

"A gun-runner and a wife-beater!" Shane mocked them both. "A real holy alliance!"

"I reckon, Preston," Woolrich sneered, "that this is the end of the trail for you."

A shaking hand lifted the rifle from Jonah's saddle holster and rested it across Tessie's saddle. Abel Sorenson's eye squinted down the sights and even as Woolrich was about to squeeze the trigger, the man in the shadows fired his gun. The bullet burned high into Matt Woolrich's chest, lifting him clean out of the saddle. Woolrich tried to level his own gun as he groped skywards, then he flopped down and his face was buried in the dust. The preacher trembled like a spring sapling as he held the smoking rifle.

Shane dropped to where his gun had fallen. Right then, Damien Blake was holding the six-shooter he'd found in Woolrich's bag, and with a yell of triumph, he lifted it to shoot. Shane rolled, scooping up his gun and firing in one swift movement. The bullet thudded between Blake's eyes and the gun-runner uttered no sound as he stared at the fading sun with dead eyes, and collapsed beside Woolrich's corpse.

Shane ran over to where Sorenson was standing, still holding the rifle.

"Thanks, Preacher," the gunfighter said soberly, relieving him of the gun and sliding it back into Jonah's saddle holster. "I reckon I owe you my life."

Sorenson looked straight at him. "All of us on that wagon train owe you our lives. I was just returning a favor."

And with that, Abel Sorenson strode away to look at possible church sites, and the tall gunfighter headed into the Golden Garter to help the wounded Jonah.

"I've come to say goodbye."

Juanita, propped up against two pillows, watched as the gunfighter closed the door behind him and walked over to her bed. He sat down beside her.

"The fort doctor says you'll be up and about in a few weeks," Shane told her. "Same as Brett Craig. He's going to live, too."

"How will Brett get on when law comes to Gun Creek?" the girl asked anxiously.

"By then, he'll be forgotten, just a small rancher somewhere west of Gun Creek. Janie told me they'll be settling farther west."

"Shane—" she whispered, "you—you *have* to leave?"

He saw the sadness in her eyes, and maybe for him, there was a sadness too.

"You know why I can't stay," he said quietly.

"Yes," she nodded, "Jonah told me all about—about your wife and why you must ride until you find the man who murdered her. Scarface, isn't it?"

"That's the man."

"Some day, when you find him—you'll ride back here?" Juanita pleaded.

"Maybe."

And looking at him, she knew that 'maybe' was all he could ever say. A man like Shane Preston couldn't predict the future for himself.

She reached out her hands and pulled his face close. Shane touched her hair and her mouth found his. The girl's full lips were soft under his.

Shane drew away from her.

"If ever I do ride back," Shane said, "then you'll probably be a married woman with a tribe of kids"

157

"And who'd have a 'breed girl who's a widow?" Juanita challenged him.

"He's waiting outside the door with a bunch of flowers in his hand," the gunfighter hinted.

"Who?" she gasped.

"Abel Sorenson," Shane stated. "Now you're a widow and no longer married to Woolrich, he's free to come courting. And that, Juanita, is precisely what he has in mind."

"Oh," she smiled.

"Juanita," he said seriously, "Abel's a damn fine man and he's taken on a big chore building a church in Gun Creek. He needs a wife to support his efforts—maybe he needs you."

Open-mouthed, she watched as Shane Preston stood up. She glanced wistfully at the strength of his shoulders, at the rugged features of his face. Shane had to move on, but he'd left something with her that time could never erase. A memory.

"Abel!" Shane called him in.

The preacher strode inside and placed the wild roses on her bedside cabinet.

"Look after her, Abel," Shane said.

Shane Preston stalked out to where the emigrants were standing around Jonah and their two horses. The gunfighter swung into the saddle and with a word to Jonah, he set his face for the fort entrance. The oldster caught up with him halfway across the parade ground, and they rode through the gates into the beckoning wilderness. The emigrants were waving to him, but as was his usual custom, Shane Preston didn't look back.

"I reckon," Jonah Jones said as he fried the beef cutlet over the campfire, "that there's one town we'll ride well clear of in the future."

"Gaucho?" Shane was leaning back on his saddle, smoking a last cigarette before Jonah finished cooking chow.

"Next time," Jonah Jones claimed, "that durn sheriff will shoot first and ask questions later."

"We'll be heading in the opposite direction to Gaucho," Shane said.

"Where's Lonegan's Well?"

"North," Shane said, opening the letter they'd collected an hour ago in Blacksmith County, their last forwarding address. "Seems like this rancher's having trouble with a bunch of hard cases."

"And he's offering us seven hundred bucks to help him out." Jonah recalled his reading of the letter.

"A lot of money," Shane mused. "But we'd ride there even if it was seven bucks."

"Like hell!" Jonah Jones spluttered indignantly, turning the cutlet before it burned.

"Fact is, Jonah," Shane said quietly, "we haven't been north before, and it'll be the first time we've ridden the country around Bearcat Mountain."

"But—for seven bucks!"

"It'll be my first chance to look for *him* north of the Snake River," Shane Preston said, flicking the ash from his cigarette tip.

Jonah said nothing, but he looked over the leaping flames at those deep impenetrable eyes and he knew what Shane Preston was thinking. Scarface could be there, not necessarily at Lonegan's Well, but somewhere north. For three years, they'd searched westwards, always hoping to meet the man he was hunting, but never finding him. Maybe all this time he was in the high country to the north, and maybe when they reached Lonegan's Well, Shane would come face to face with his quarry. And then, Jonah told himself, his pard would kill for the last time. But perhaps after the job at Lonegan's Well, they would ride away and Scarface would still be living and enjoying life. If this should happen, then Shane and Jonah would continue to hire out their guns to defend the oppressed and to earn enough money to keep riding.

Suddenly there was a strong aroma of scorched flesh.

"Great fires of hell!" Jonah Jones cursed as he looked down at the burnt offering in the pan.

"If I ever settle down," Shane said wryly, "remind me never to hire you on as cook!"